BURNING UNCLE TOM'S CABIN

BURNING UNCLE TOM'S CABIN SERIES

CARL WATERS

DR. KAL CHINYERE

Bright Sons

ISBN: 978-1-939805-00-3

For my daughter, Zoë

It is better to take what does not belong to you than to let it lie around neglected.

— MARK TWAIN

GET YOUR FREE STORY!

Go to the link below and get your free copy of the story, *The Runaway Slave Returns*. It's a prequel to *Burning Uncle Tom's Cabin*.

www.BrightSons.com/RSRFree

INTRODUCTION

My original plan was to produce a young adult dystopian novel about a post-Second Civil War United States that had been taken over by an extreme political group. After the war, the group would have revoked the Thirteenth Amendment and re-enslaved African Americans.

To help get my head in the best space for my ambitious task, I chose numerous nonfiction sources for my slavery research. I also chose to reread Harriet Beecher Stowe's *Uncle Tom's Cabin*, Margaret Mitchell's *Gone with the Wind*, and Toni Morrison's *Beloved*.

Of the novels, I read *Uncle Tom's Cabin* first.

Uncle Tom's Cabin is arguably the most influential novel in the history of the United States. Stowe's book was the best-selling novel of the nineteenth century. It changed the way hundreds of thousands of people around the world viewed slavery. In particular, *Uncle Tom's Cabin* was extremely beneficial to the abolitionist cause. Stowe's forward-thinking views on slavery showed her courage as an active abolitionist, and by writing *Uncle Tom's Cabin*, she showed even more courage.

Interestingly, while Stowe was progressive in her views on race, this was only relative to other white people at the time. After reading more of her work, including *A Key to Uncle Tom's Cabin*—a nonfiction companion to the novel—it is obvious that she believed black people had souls and that slavery was wrong. However, she also believed black people were inferior to white people. These beliefs shine through in her stereotypical characters, and they are unknowingly damaging to new readers of her work, both black and non-black. Even so, the United States is forever in her debt because of how her fiction humanized an entire race of people and eventually helped change our nation's politics.

Before rereading *Uncle Tom's Cabin*, I didn't remember much about the story, which I first read as a child. I only remembered that—spoiler alert!—Uncle Tom died. Reading the book as an adult was eye-opening, and I have to admit that I now have mixed feelings about it.

After rereading *Uncle Tom's Cabin*, my lasting thought is that

Uncle Tom, the main character in the novel, isn't an "Uncle Tom" in the derogatory sense that the term is used today. He does not betray or turn his back on the other African American characters to benefit the white ones.

Do not get me wrong. I am not a fan of Uncle Tom as a character, but I do understand that he was created and shaped in Stowe's mind to help abolish slavery by increasing sympathies toward the plights of slaves. I do not understand or agree with Uncle Tom's overall mindset. I definitely do not understand or agree with Uncle Tom's refusal to immediately take his freedom when it is offered to him by Augustine St. Clare. However, Uncle Tom's thoughts and actions aren't based on him being a race trai-tor. Uncle Tom's thoughts and actions, instead, are based on his personal interpretation of the Bible and Christianity. He never once betrayed another slave. He actually did the opposite. By not running away, he sacrificed himself to save other slaves on the Shelby plantation, and he didn't betray the slave Eliza Harris after her unlawful escape.

Further, Uncle Tom is murdered for refusing to betray Cassy and Emmeline, two runaway slaves. Uncle Tom is, at worst, simpleminded. But he is no "Uncle Tom."

After finishing the novel, I wished that I could go into Stowe's world and save Uncle Tom from himself and from

Simon Legree. Then I decided to stop wishing and just do it. The bigger questions then became, who would save Uncle Tom, and how would they do it? I have decided that these questions should be answered by another character from *Uncle Tom's Cabin*, George Harris.

While I dislike and feel sorry for Uncle Tom, I love George Harris. George is a disgruntled slave who refuses to accept that he is inferior to his enslavers. He also refuses to accept that he has to be a slave. George is a fighter who fights his way to freedom. In Carl and I's revisionist take, George is the perfect person to rescue Uncle Tom.

All the thoughts I had after reading *Uncle Tom's Cabin* have led to my own take on a classic American novel. In the *Burning Uncle Tom's Cabin* series, Uncle Tom faces a different fate than the one Stowe granted him. The "Burning" in the title is meant to symbolize my attempt to destroy the negative and stereotypical African American images found in the original *Uncle Tom's Cabin*.

The *Burning Uncle Tom's Cabin* series comprises at least ten books whose narratives are told from the slaves' points of view. Carl Waters and I have removed many of the racial stereotypes, plot holes, and excessive preaching from Harriet Beecher Stowe's world-changing story.

Burning Uncle Tom's Cabin is the first book in the series. It is the story of George and Eliza Harris told from their points of view. Uncle Tom is a minor character in this novel, but he will be a major character in subsequent novels. In Book One, we did not stray far from the story of the original *Uncle Tom's Cabin*. This will not be the case in future stories.

— Kalvin C. Chinyere, MD, MBA (Dr. Kal)

CHAPTER 1

February 21, 1851

Georg Harris looked up at the sky, his mood suddenly turning sour. The day around him couldn't have been more beautiful: a clear, crystal blue sky with nary a cloud in it, a gentle breeze, and the company of the people he loved most dearly—his wife Eliza and his son Harry. There were winter bushes blooming in the tree line —witch hazel and dogwoods, with their bright yellows and reds against the dulled grass—and many of the trees still held their leaves. All told, he knew he should have been quite happy.

And yet…and yet.

"George, must you go back so soon?" Eliza asked, her eyes full of both doubt and pleading.

George sighed and nodded in resignation. As much as he hated it, he did have to go back to the factory, and there was nothing for it. Although life in the factory—where his owner, Frank Harris, had sent him to work—gave him more freedom than he would have had on a plantation, that freedom was fleeting. He'd secured the afternoon off to come to this picnic with his family, but time was short—and he'd come to the end of it. The truth was, he wasn't able to make his own decisions today, or any other day, and back to the factory he had to go.

"Now Eliza, you know as well as I that I can't stay," he said gently, reaching out to touch her cheek.

"But Papa!" Harry cried, running toward the couple and throwing his arms around George's neck. "Why do you have to go? Why can't you stay here with Mamma and me?"

George took the little boy's arms and unwound them, pushing them slowly back to the solid little lad's sides. "Harry, I must go do the work I'm bid to do, and when you're older, you'll understand. A man must do his job after all, must he not?"

The little boy, who looked so much like his mother with his long ringlets and smooth skin that George marveled to see it, firmed his childlike mouth and straightened his shoulders, nodding sternly. George smiled; the boy would be a fine man one day. Years and years in the future. And perhaps—he hoped—in another world entirely.

"You'll be a good man and see to your mother, won't you?" he asked softly. "Make sure she gets home safely, as the man of the family while I'm away?"

At this the little boy's lower lip began to quiver, and his firm resolve melted away. "I don't understand why you can't stay, Papa. Mas'r Shelby always stays with Missis Shelby. Why must you leave us?"

George glanced at Eliza, his eyebrows raised in question. How were they to explain that to their son? Arthur and Emily Shelby were the owners of the plantation, after all, and a far cry from George and Eliza, who were little more than overeducated slaves. George and Eliza had some freedom, to be sure—Eliza the favorite of the house and George a factory worker in town. But their small freedoms were nothing like those of the master and mistress.

Eliza lifted one shoulder in mute response, then called little Harry over to her. "Your father's the only one who knows how to run the factory, little one. He must go, you see, or the factory can't run rightly. You'll understand when you're older."

"When he's older, perhaps he won't have to understand such things," George muttered, staring at the ground. "By that time, we'll be far away from here, and free as the day is long."

"George, don't talk that way," Eliza reprimanded him. "You know I don't like it, and your son's prone to repeatin' what he hears. You want him to say that sort o' thing to the wrong people?"

At that, he relented. She was right, and he would never forgive himself if he caused trouble for his family before he was ready. Before he had his plans in place. Another month or so—that was all he needed. Until then, he would have to keep his head down, and he needed his son to do the same. "Harry," he called to his son. The boy ran back to him, his arms spread and the tears clear in his eyes, and fell into George's lap.

"We're a family, though we might not spend as much time together as the Shelbys," George murmured. "We're just different, that's all. Your mother and I must live in different places—for our work, you see—but we love each other very much. You must never forget that. And you must never forget how much I love you, and how much I love your mother. We'll be together soon, and that's a promise."

"A promise, Papa?" the boy asked, looking winsomely up at George.

"A promise," George agreed firmly. He leaned forward to

plant a kiss firmly between Harry's eyes, gave the boy a cross-eyed look of affection, and then put him from his lap. "Eliza, I'll be back as soon as I can," he said, taking her into his arms and kissing her soundly. He leaned back to gaze at her, remembering the day they'd first met. He'd been sent to the factory to work, courtesy of his master, and she'd been in town on an errand for her mistress. George had taken one look at her wide eyes and long, curling hair, her lips that turned out in a pout when she was upset, and knew that he was stuck.

When he spoke to Eliza and found that a fire burned in her soul, George knew that he must be with her. They'd lived separately for some years now, with different masters, but they still saw each other regularly, although never often enough. And never for as long as he'd wish. Saying good-bye to her...it never became easier.

"I pray you'll think of me at night, and come when I call you," he whispered, leaning forward and resting his fore-head against hers.

"Always, George," she whispered. "Come back to us soon."

With a quick nod, he rose, turned on his heel, and headed for the road, his heart aching at the life that forced him to leave his wife and child behind.

CHAPTER 2

George put one foot in front of the other on the trail, willing himself back to the factory, though he left his heart behind him. Around him, the oranges and yellows of the witch hazel taunted him, the cheerful faces turned up to the watery winter sun as if they wanted nothing else, and the leaves of the trees blew softly in the breeze, adding their rustle to the sounds of the clear day. The scrub and dogwood rustled as well, scratching against the trunks of the trees, and one or two birds whistled in the sunshine.

George, angry at having had to leave his family and growing angrier with every step he took, suddenly couldn't stand the happy flowers any longer. How dare they live their satisfied lives, free to bloom as they pleased, when he—a man—didn't have the right to do anything? He darted into the brush and began ripping the flowers from their stems, throwing them around in a show of sheer temper. He shouted in frustration and kicked at the nearest tree. Anything—anything—to make some sort of impression on the world around him. To leave a sign that he had been here. To make some sort of difference.

All he managed to do, however, was stub his toe and soil his hands with the flowers.

Annoyed, deeply unsatisfied with his momentary temper tantrum, and realizing that anyone who saw him would brand him insane, he stumbled back out to the road and continued on his way. He was particularly blue at having left Eliza and Harry behind once again. Though the freedoms of his work as the assistant foreman at the hemp factory were unheard of for a slave, it still kept him from his wife and child more often than he would like. It might be three days or another week before he'd have time to see them again, and that didn't sit well with him.

George was a slave, and that didn't sit well with him either. Despite his intelligence and ingenuity, white men still dictated his days and nights and what work he was and was not allowed to do. They told him when to eat and sleep, whom he could marry, and how often he'd be allowed to see her. In short, they told him how to live his life.

His situation was far from unique. Most of the Negroes in Kentucky were slaves. George had never even met a free

Negro though he'd heard the rumors about their existence. But for as long as he could remember, the world around him hadn't changed. And beyond his own memories, his people's history told him that it had been this way for the descendants of the Africans for hundreds of years.

That didn't make it right.

He growled and put the argument away for the time being. It wasn't the first time he'd thought such things, and he knew it wouldn't be the last. For the moment, however, he needed to focus on getting back to the factory before he was missed; he was important to the foreman, but that wouldn't save him from punishment if he was gone too long. At the thought, he quickened his pace, lengthened his strides under the swaying oak and willow trees, and estimated how much farther he had left.

"Best appreciate what you have, George," he told himself sternly, seeking to turn his train of thought to something more positive. "You're one of the only slaves 'round as gets to spend time with his wife and child at all, let alone take an entire weekday afternoon." He heaved another sigh, then looked up. The edge of town had come into sight on the road ahead, and there the hemp factory stood, no more than half a mile away.

He smiled then, despite himself, and his heart warmed at

the sight of his place of work. "Only slave 'round as gets to do something he loves too. Best be thankful for what you got, stop moaning 'bout what you don't." With that, he walked forward more quickly, toward the hemp-bagging factory that had been his home for nearly five years.

George hadn't chosen to work in the place. His master, Frank Harris, had rented him out to the factory when many of the factory's slaves died from an illness. It hadn't been a selfless gesture, nor had it been done for the income of renting out a slave. Not really. Harris' plantation produced hemp, and the hemp factory purchased most of it. If they didn't have enough men to work, the factory wouldn't buy Harris' hemp.

George hadn't been expecting much when he started at the factory. It had seemed just another example of Harris dictating his life. But he'd quickly discovered that he enjoyed the work there—enjoyed the freedom of working for a man that didn't own him outright. That freedom had become even greater some months earlier when he'd invented a machine that cleaned the hemp on its own, doing the work of several men—and more quickly, saving the factory both time and money.

Before he knew it, George was at the entrance to the factory, stepping through the front door. Toward the back of the first room, he saw the foreman, Charles Wilson, standing in front of the hemp-cleaning machine George had invented. The man was gesturing grandly, throwing his arms out as he showed the machine to another man who stood with his back to the entrance.

George smiled to himself. Wilson had been incredibly impressed with the invention when George presented it, and took the opportunity to brag about it as often as he could. In fact, he could hear the man's voice now, raised in excitement and enthusiasm.

"You wouldn't believe it, man, how quickly it works! Saves us the work o' many men, and no mistake!" he was saying.

George hastened toward them, weaving through the bags of hemp on the floor and watching his step in the dim lighting. "Mr. Wilson, no one finds it as fascinatin' as you do," he said from behind them, laughing.

Wilson turned, laughing as well. "Well now, George, credit where credit is due, and you deserve every bit of it. I've just been showin' it to Mr. Harris himself, tellin' him how lucky he is to have a man such as you at his biddin'."

George's eyes widened in shock and horror, and he whipped his head toward the other man. Mr. Harris? The very man he'd never wanted to see again. The man he'd thought to be a stranger turned toward him as well, revealing a displeased, arrogant look on his face, long as a horse's and twice as ugly, but secure in its importance to the world. The body was tall and gangly, and he certainly knew the set of those shoulders. Yes, this was indeed Harris, and George's heart sank at the thought. His master, then, come to check on him as if he'd heard George's very thoughts about freedom.

"Impressive indeed, George," the man said, his tone conveying that he was anything but impressed. "Though I tell you right now, I can see why you'd do it. Plain as day, it is, and only one reason for a Negro to invent such a thing—save himself work, Wilson, and no more than that. Surprised you didn't see it yourself, in fact," he muttered, sliding a cruel glance in Wilson's direction.

George gasped and shook his head fiercely. "No sir, not a'tall. Cleans the hemp for us, y'see, gives the men time to move on to more important work, so that we—"

"Don't make no difference, boy, and what're you thinkin', contradictin' your superior like that? I see you been gettin' airs about you, just as I feared you would." With that, Harris turned sharply toward Wilson, who stood with a shocked and dismayed look on his face.

"Can't say I appreciate your treatment of my boy, Wilson, allowin' him to take on airs in that manner. Ain't good for the boy, a thing like that. Fact is, I came here today to take him home with me. Think he's spent about enough time at this here factory, dealin' with these newfangled machines." Harris' foot shot out and gave the hemp-cleaning machine a sharp blow. George stifled another gasp.

Wilson put a protective hand on the machine and turned to stare at Harris. "Why, what can you mean, Mr. Harris?" he sputtered. "Take the man home? Why would you do such a thing when he's well suited for work here? Why, he's already saved me hundreds o' dollars with this here invention, and you're collectin' his salary, aren't you? On top o' what we pay you for the loan o' the man?"

Shocked himself, George put out a hand to stop the foreman and turned to Harris. "Mas'r Harris, take me home? Surely you can't mean—"

"I do mean, boy, and you'd do well to remember who's master here. What I say goes, and well you know it," Harris snarled. He raised a hand, threatening to strike George, and scowled heavily.

George opened his mouth and closed it again, horrified. He'd spent almost five years working at this factory, building his position and refining the process, flexing his creativity with the machinery, doing everything he could to make the factory run more smoothly though he never saw a dime from it. And now Harris meant to take him away—for his own pleasure? "But why?" he whispered. "I never did anything important at the farm, and I'm helpin' here. There's no reason for me to return to the plantation."

Instead of answering, Harris flew forward, wrapped his hand in George's shirt, and pulled him sharply forward. He shoved his own face into George's. "I've had about enough of your lip, boy," he snarled. "I see you've learned to take yourself too seriously here, and I won't have it, you hear me? That's enough out of you. You'll receive a lash for every word you say from here on out, so you'll keep your mouth shut if'n you know what's good for you."

Wilson stepped in now, much to George's relief, and put his hand on Harris' arm. "Mr. Harris, this is quite sudden. If it's a matter o' compensation, I'd be happy to pay more. George…well, he's suited for this business, sir, as I've said. I've never seen mechanical genius like his, and I'd sure hate to lose him."

"I don't need more compensation for him, Wilson!" Harris shouted, turning on the foreman. "Fact is, he's my man. I own him, don't I? And I'll do what I want with him."

"But Mr. Harris—" Wilson began.

"That's enough, Mr. Wilson!" Harris roared. "I won't have him stayin' another minute, pickin' up airs and thinkin' too high of himself! This boy's a lazy, no-good Negro, ain't never done anything worthwhile at my plantation! I tell you, he's just invented this machine to save himself work! And I have to hear it from my neighbors, that this here slave's the smartest you ever seen, smarter than a white man even! I hear he's goin' back and forth to the Shelby plantation, often as he pleases, free as the wind. I hear he's puttin' on airs, thinkin' himself very high 'n mighty. And I been told I'm lettin' my slaves act too free, same as Shelby himself. I'm lettin' my slaves act too free when it's your doin', Mr. Wilson! Well, I tell you, I've had enough—enough of the boy's attitude and enough of your braggin'! I won't let you make a fool of me anymore. I've come to take him back to the plantation. We're returnin' tonight, and I won't hear another word!"

Wilson drew a breath, taken aback at this sudden eruption, and George drew himself up, trying desperately to think of a way to right this ship. He couldn't go home, not now. In a month or so—thirty days!—he was meant to be leaving this place. Before he could say anything, though, Harris had turned back to him, his eyes glowing with hatred.

"Get to your room, boy, and gather your things. We're leavin' immediately." He turned to Wilson, still snarling. "I'll take the boy's owed wages, Wilson, and don't expect him to come back here again."

Wilson nodded once. "Well, Mr. Harris, he is your man, and

I'll respect your right to take him back. But I hope you'll consider sending him here again if you ever think of it. Come, I'll count out his remainin' wages in the office." He shot one sorrowful look George's way and shook his head. "George, you'd best do as your master tells you. Pack your things. We'll be waitin' at the front entrance."

The two white men turned toward the office and walked stiffly away, leaving George to his own devices. George, seeing that the decision was quite made and that he had no further say in the matter, turned and slipped toward his room, his heart hammering in his chest. One month. That's all he'd needed. And now all his planning was for naught.

~

He looked around the room when he arrived, his mind running quickly through the time he'd spent here. Five years he'd lived in this room. Five years he'd spent dreaming and planning in that bed, thinking about where he'd go and what he'd do. There was the bookshelf above his bed where he kept his hoard of carefully selected books. And there, the desk where he'd spent so many hours planning and drawing out the machine he'd built. Two other machines lay on those papers—drawings only, for now, but he'd thought to bring them to life after his escape.

And below them, the ciphered notes he'd made about how to get away from this place for good.

"All for nothing now, isn't it, Carlo?" he asked, ducking down to the floor where his puppy—a gift from Eliza—lay napping. George looked down at the dog, his heart breaking.

"Looks like we'll be sleeping somewhere else tonight, boy, and I can't promise it'll be any better than this." He glanced around once more at the tidy space. It had been his own, and he'd kept it the way he wanted—neat and clean, an escape from the real world. Where they were going, on the other hand…

"In fact, I can tell you it'll be worse," he finished, remembering the plantation where he'd grown up: dirty cabins, rising before dawn, mindless labor through the day—an end to his access to books and little to no opportunity for him to grow his plans.

"And no more picnics with Eliza and Harry, I can guarantee that," he muttered, half to himself and half to the dog. Eliza's home was here, near town, with the Shelby family. The Harris plantation was a full five miles away, and George knew for certain that Harris wouldn't give him leave to visit. But that was how it was here, in the United States. The land of the free. George snorted at the label, for this land would never be free. Not for someone like him.

"Nothin' for it now, Carlo old boy," he murmured, rubbing the dog's ears one last time and then moving firmly toward the bed to start packing his things. "Canada or nothing. Only way I'm ever goin' to be free. It'll be harder to get away now—but it doesn't mean it won't happen."

CHAPTER 3

George threw another flat stone across the water, slinging it sideways so that it skipped across the surface, and laughed aloud when it went farther than the last. Days like this, when he'd been up since dawn and out in the cold fields all day, tilling the frozen earth, he had to take his pleasures in the simple things.

"Six skips, Carlo, how 'bout that one?" he chortled, looking down at the puppy next to him. The dog looked up, his tongue lolling out in a grin, as if he was nearly as pleased at his master's progress as the man himself.

George's eyes traveled from the pup's face to his ribcage, and his smile fell. The dog had been just this side of chubby when they lived at the factory, living on George's scraps and unfinished meals, and the other workers had passed their

time sneaking pieces of dried meat to the dog. Now, after a few weeks on the plantation, Carlo was already starting to look thinner, his weight melting away with the lack of food and increased stress.

George dropped to his knees next to the dog, taking his head in his hands and staring into his eyes. "I know it ain't what it used to be, Carlo, but I promise it'll get better. Can't live this way for much longer myself." He stood and skipped two more stones in quick succession, his thoughts growing angrier with each passing moment.

Since he'd returned to the plantation, he'd been forced into manual labor, Harris finding ever more mindless tasks for the slave with the brilliant mind. George had worked in the fields for the first fews day, his hands blistering with the unfamiliar work, and he had then been moved into the stables, where he was told to muck the stalls and scrub the wooden floors and walls. Today he'd been back out in the fields, the frozen wind screaming up his back and cutting through his too-thin clothing.

It hadn't taken long to remember how much he'd hated life here.

"Miss the factory, do ya, Carlo?" he asked, throwing another stone. "Well, so do I. Miss the company, miss the work, miss

the fact that they treated me like a man rather than an animal…" He stopped to throw Carlo an ironic glance at that and muttered, "No offense, 'course."

Still, not even joking with his dog could ease his mind of the ache that had been growing in his heart. Harris had assigned him the worst work on the plantation, and he knew what it meant: Harris would have it out for him from here on. No more small freedoms, no more intellectual leanings, and certainly no speaking out of turn.

And, what was worse, no more time spent with Eliza or Harry. No more time with his family. The simplest and purest pleasure any man could take—the company of those he loved—and it was completely gone.

"Already told me not to expect to see them no more," he noted quietly, speaking half to himself and half to the dog. "'Bout broke my heart when he said that, Carlo. But I won't let him stop me—you mark my words. I won't let him tell me how to live. I'll find a way out of this, and I'll take y'all with me." He firmed his jaw, remembering his plans for Canada, and was about to expand on those thoughts when he heard a noise behind him.

"Who you talkin' to, boy?" a voice asked harshly.

George jumped and whirled around, recognizing the voice.

"Just talkin' to myself, Mas'r," he mumbled, praying that Harris hadn't heard what he'd said. Talking about disobeying the master was worth a beating, and talking about something like freedom was worth much worse.

When he turned, he saw—to his shock—that not only Harris but also his son, little Frank, and the overseer William Henry stood behind him. How long had they been there? Had they heard what he said? His mind raced, trying to recall exactly what he'd said and how much trouble he might be in.

"What're you doin' out here, boy?" Harris asked, narrowing his eyes in suspicion.

"Finished with work for the day, sir," George answered, fighting not to narrow his own eyes in return. What were these three doing checking on him so late in the evening? The day was over, and his time was his own after dinner, according to the rules of the plantation.

Of course, he realized suddenly, the rules could change according to Harris' mood.

"You ain't finished 'til I say you're finished, boy, and you ought to know that by now," Harris snarled, confirming George's worst fears. "You ain't at the factory no more, makin' your own schedule or your own rules."

"I didn't make any rules, sir, just did my job," George said quietly, staring hard at the ground. "Mr. Wilson trusted me, is all." Talking back to the master was a bad idea, he knew, but he couldn't seem to help it—the man had a way of getting under George's skin so that he felt he must defend himself, come hell or high water.

Harris strode slowly toward him, laughing to himself. "Wilson came by earlier, matter of fact," he said. "Lookin' for you, askin' if I'd send you back. Told him I'd shoot him for trespassin', he ever set foot on my land again. Ain't gonna see that man again. Fact is, boy, it's time you realized you're nothin' more than a slave. Time for you to come to terms with your place in life."

At that, George's head shot up, his temper coming suddenly to the fore. "I'm a man, same as you are," he spat, too angry to keep quiet.

Harris narrowed his eyes again, matching George's hatred. "Time you were broken of those thoughts, boy," he spat back. "The sooner you realize your place, the better." He grabbed George's arm and shook him roughly until Carlo barked in surprise and defense, springing to his feet and charging at the man he now recognized as the enemy.

George put out a hand to stop him, but it was already too late, for the foreman had shot forward and grabbed Carlo

George watched in horror as William and young Frank tossed the helpless puppy into the deep water, the stone at his neck. There the dog struggled for a moment, thrashing wildly in the water, his eyes on George who stared into Carlo's gaze, noting the sorrow and confusion—the absolute terror—in his eyes.

"Let me save him," he yelled, pulling against Harris. "Let me go to him!"

Harris merely laughed and watched as the dog sank under the water, finally disappearing altogether. When the water stilled over Carlo, Harris released George and took a step back.

"Now your work is done, George, and I suggest that you remember what I can do to you when I put my mind to it."

George dropped to his knees and stared at the spot where his dog had disappeared, his vision blurring with angry tears.

∼

Sometime later, George made his way back to the men's slave quarters, noting quietly how lonely and dark it had become now that Carlo was gone. He sank heavily onto

George watched in horror as William and young Frank tossed the helpless puppy into the deep water, the stone at his neck. There the dog struggled for a moment, thrashing wildly in the water, his eyes on George who stared into Carlo's gaze, noting the sorrow and confusion—the absolute terror—in his eyes.

"Let me save him," he yelled, pulling against Harris. "Let me go to him!"

Harris merely laughed and watched as the dog sank under the water, finally disappearing altogether. When the water stilled over Carlo, Harris released George and took a step back.

"Now your work is done, George, and I suggest that you remember what I can do to you when I put my mind to it."

George dropped to his knees and stared at the spot where his dog had disappeared, his vision blurring with angry tears.

~

Sometime later, George made his way back to the men's slave quarters, noting quietly how lonely and dark it had become now that Carlo was gone. He sank heavily onto

George's heart stopped, then started hammering away again. "What?" he gasped. "I would never! I will never do such a thing, Mas'r Harris. That dog was a gift from my wife!"

"If you won't do it, I'll do it for you, boy," Harris muttered. He threw a glance at the foreman and then at his son. "William, you give that dog to my son there. Frank, you're to tie a stone around that dog's neck—the heaviest one you can find—and throw him into the water, hear me?"

George froze, not allowing himself to comprehend Harris' words, and saw with horror that the boy—only ten, but already just as cruel as his father—was in fact doing this very thing. The foreman held the dog down while the boy tied a heavy rock to the rope at his neck, then helped the youngster carry the puppy—yelping and struggling—toward the pond.

"No!" George shouted, his voice breaking. He turned away, unwilling to watch, but Harris forced him back around, holding his chin so that he couldn't look away.

"You'll watch, boy, and you'll learn your lesson. This is what happens to things that you love. Everything you have belongs to me, and I'll do with it as I wish. Throw that dog in!" he shouted.

by the rope around his neck. Harris' eyes traveled toward the dog, shining with a sly sort of cunning, and his lips turned up.

"Seen you with that dog, boy, feedin' him from your own plate," he said, his gaze turning sharp.

"Only fed him kitchen scraps, Mas'r Harris, ain't no rule against that!" George said, struggling against the master's grip. Before him, he could see Carlo pulling desperately against the rope, his eyes panicked at the tense atmosphere.

"Those scraps're for the pigs, not your dog, boy, and I won't have it." Harris paused, the air around them thick with hatred and malice. "Matter of fact, think that dog's costin' me money, which means you're costing me money. You're feedin' him at my expense, ain't you?"

"Dog don't eat hardly anything, Mas'r, he's not doin' any harm," George moaned, already afraid of where this was going.

Harris shook him firmly. "He is doin' harm, and we'll be done with him today. This pond'll help me solve two problems at once. You'll drown that dog of yours, George, and you'll do it now. Teach you your place. Teach you to take orders when you should."

"I didn't make any rules, sir, just did my job," George said quietly, staring hard at the ground. "Mr. Wilson trusted me, is all." Talking back to the master was a bad idea, he knew, but he couldn't seem to help it—the man had a way of getting under George's skin so that he felt he must defend himself, come hell or high water.

Harris strode slowly toward him, laughing to himself. "Wilson came by earlier, matter of fact," he said. "Lookin' for you, askin' if I'd send you back. Told him I'd shoot him for trespassin', he ever set foot on my land again. Ain't gonna see that man again. Fact is, boy, it's time you realized you're nothin' more than a slave. Time for you to come to terms with your place in life."

At that, George's head shot up, his temper coming suddenly to the fore. "I'm a man, same as you are," he spat, too angry to keep quiet.

Harris narrowed his eyes again, matching George's hatred. "Time you were broken of those thoughts, boy," he spat back. "The sooner you realize your place, the better." He grabbed George's arm and shook him roughly until Carlo barked in surprise and defense, springing to his feet and charging at the man he now recognized as the enemy.

George put out a hand to stop him, but it was already too late, for the foreman had shot forward and grabbed Carlo the thin pallet, and gazed into the water in the bucket on the floor, staring into his own guilt-ridden eyes. He'd always thought himself a well-favored man, tall and handsome, smarter than most and quick to learn. But none of that had saved him from this tragedy or the life into which he'd been born. He was unable to see his family. Unable to do his work. Told not to use his mind. And now, his dog had been drowned before his eyes, with him helpless to do anything to stop it. As he thought about it, his sorrow began to turn to anger, and soon his reflection in the water showed nothing so much as the glowing of his temper.

That man had no right to treat him—a human being!—in this way. Who had made Harris any better than George himself? Who had said that he was a better, more favored man than George? No one had. No one but the laws of this forsaken country.

The laws of this country would rule him as long as he lived here. As long as he was in the country, he'd have to obey them. And as long as those laws were in place and Harris could do as he wanted…

"Eliza and Harry," George murmured, suddenly realizing what else Harris could take from him. He would have trouble doing that—after all, Eliza and Harry belonged to another man—but he could stop George from seeing them.

In fact, he was already trying to do just that. And as long as George belonged to him, according to the law…

"I'll do anything. I must to keep seeing them," he said then, to no one in particular. "Be as obedient as I must. Give Harris no reason to hate me. Work as hard as possible. Until the day I escape."

CHAPTER 4

After a few days, George saw his first opportunity to impress his new attitude upon the master. He'd just finished cleaning out the stable and saw when he came out that Harris was sitting on the porch of his house, the slave woman Mina waiting on his needs. Harris had a carafe of coffee sitting next to him on the table and was sipping slowly at a cup of it, looking out over the cold, crisp winter day. The world around them was indeed bright and clear—sharp in the way that only a winter sun could cast it—with a soft dusting of snow on the ground from the night before. The air should have been cold but was warm enough for comfort, and a shaft of sunlight had managed to cut through the sky to highlight Harris himself.

George, realizing that this was the ideal time, straightened his shoulders and walked briskly through the warm winter air toward the porch.

"Nice day out, Mas'r," he said quietly, climbing the steps and glancing from Mina to Harris. "Glad to see you're able to sit and enjoy the sun."

"Can't imagine workin' on a day like this, boy. Days like these're made for sittin' and drinkin' coffee. Admirin' the sunshine."

"Well, we're here to work on these days so gentlemen like you don't need to," George answered, hating the words as they came out of his mouth. *For Eliza and Harry*, he told himself sternly. *You're doing this for them.*

Harris shook his cup—now empty—at Mina, and she scuttled forward to fill it again, throwing George a shocked and somewhat dismayed look. George met her eyes once, understanding her look, and hated himself a bit more for what he was saying.

"Sounds like you're finally startin' to understand your place, boy," Harris said in a satisfied tone, as if he'd worked hard to show George the light.

George bit the inside of his lip, gave Mina a slow wink, and arranged his features so that Harris wouldn't see the rebellion in his heart. "I do, sir, you're right about that," he answered slowly. "I've been working very hard of late—harder and longer than anyone else—and I hope you'll be proud of me."

Harris grunted. "Foreman told me as much. Can't say I'm proud, George, but I'm pleased, and that should be enough for you."

George paused. Now was the time. He'd come for a reason, and he couldn't put it off any longer. "Wondered if I could go see my wife and son, Mas'r, now that I'm workin' so hard. Not until Sunday, of course. Won't go until our day off."

"No," Harris snapped.

"But sir—"

"I said no, boy! I won't have no slave of mine at the Shelby plantation. That highfalutin' Shelby didn't give us no support for the Fugitive Slave Act; good as told us all that if a slave runs off we should let them go! Didn't make no friends, I can tell you that much, and I won't have you associatin' with any of his people. Don't want no dealin's with that man."

George drew back as if he'd been slapped. He'd known that Harris could forbid him from seeing Eliza and Harry, of course, but he'd hoped it wouldn't come to that. "But Mas'r, that's my wife and child," he began.

"No, that's Shelby's girl and boy."

"But—"

"You're finished with them, George, and that's that. I won't have my best man wastin' his seed on a girl belongs to that turncoat Shelby, givin' that plantation big strong children when I need them here!" He paused, eyeing the woman at his side, and then grinned evilly. "Fact, think I'll put you with Mina here. Get me some big, strong children of my own."

George opened his mouth and closed it again, almost too shocked to answer. "What?" he gasped.

Mina dropped the fan, her own face a mask of horror. She turned to stare at George, her eyes pleading with him to do something. She couldn't want this any more than he did, he knew—being forced to bed a man without love and have his children just because the master said so. Because she'd been in the wrong place at the wrong time.

But George was too concerned with his own sense of loss to spend much time thinking of Mina's. "I can't do that, Mas'r Harris. I'm already a married man," he stuttered.

Harris turned to him, his eyes full of malice. "You want to see your wife? I'll have William take you over there right now, boy. Tell that girl you won't be goin' over there no more. She's welcome here, if Shelby'll sell her. If he won't, you'll never see her again." He turned away from George and motioned for Mina to refill his coffee cup, as if the conversation was done and settled.

"But—" George started again, his temper mounting. Wasn't this just what he'd been thinking to himself for years now? That this man would try to tell him how to live his life—and succeed in doing so—just because the laws of this godforsaken country gave him the right?

This time Harris didn't even bother looking at him. "I'm only lettin' you go to say good-bye because I know it'll upset Shelby, but one more word, boy, and I'll go tell Shelby myself."

George spun on his heel, forcing himself down the steps and across the lawn before his temper emerged. His heart sat broken in his chest at the thought of what Harris was trying to do—keep him from his Eliza and force him to marry another woman! Force him to impregnate that woman, to produce children for Harris to abuse. He would never do it, never!

But if he couldn't see his family, there was no reason to stay.

He'd meant to leave Kentucky on a Saturday night, when he'd first started planning. It would have been the ideal time. The factory is always closed on Sundays, and no one would have missed him until the following Monday morning. Of course those plans had disappeared like smoke when

Harris brought him back to the plantation. He'd still thought to go, but not until he saw his opening.

Now, he realized, Harris was forcing his hand. He'd go to Eliza tonight, as Harris had demanded. He'd tell her what he'd been planning. And he'd make her see that he had to leave.

CHAPTER 5

Eliza threw aside the curtains, scanning the yard outside desperately for her son. Harry had taken to hiding from her of late, and though the child thought it was all good fun and giggled mercilessly whenever she found him, Eliza dreaded these moments.

The more rational part of her mind reminded her that she always found him and that he couldn't have gone far. The emotional side of her, however, reminded her of the two children she miscarried and the fact that as a slave, she could never tell what might happen, even to her own child. She'd known too many women who had come home to find their children missing, sold to a trader, never to return.

In short, she hated the days when her son decided to play hide-and-seek.

What made the whole thing worse was that she hadn't seen

her husband in weeks—not since their picnic when he'd brought food for her and Harry and upset her with his plan to run away to Canada and take her and Harry with him. She hadn't seen or heard from him since. Luckily, Wilson—his foreman at the factory—had stopped by the Shelby plantation to tell her what had happened. Harris had heard of George's invention and success at the factory and gone to take him back, Wilson said, and there had been no talking the man out of it. Wilson had gone to the Harris plantation to seek George once again, asking if he might come back to the factory.

In short, Harris had told Wilson never to set foot on his property again, at the risk of being shot.

"I'm afraid his mind is set, miss," Wilson told her. "George won't be comin' back to the factory, and I tell you, I don't know what Harris means to do with him. But I'm sure it can be nothin' good." With those fatalistic words, he'd taken his leave. Eliza had watched him go, her heart breaking at the thought of it.

Not go back to the factory? Stuck at the Harris plantation, doing who knew what? That meant he was over five miles away—and without the freedom to come see her. She hadn't heard from him since he'd gone back, and now she started to fear that she'd never hear from him again.

Harry hiding away today—and making her feel as if she'd lost him as well—was the final straw.

She turned, distraught, and rushed down to the kitchen. Aunt Chloe, the cook, had been baking cookies earlier, and perhaps that had drawn Harry. Eliza burst through the door, but saw nothing out of the ordinary in the kitchen. The big oven sat dormant against the opposite wall, its burners all empty and cool. The counter alongside it held stacks and stacks of cookies—enough to feed the entire plantation, she thought—all out on cooling racks. On the other side of the room, Aunt Chloe and her husband, the foreman Uncle Tom, sat in front of the fireplace, bent down over a book of some sort. They looked up when Eliza rushed in, their faces wearing similar expressions of surprise and puzzlement.

"Why Lizzie, what ails you, girl?" Aunt Chloe asked.

Eliza leaned against the doorway, her chest heaving. "I'm lookin' for Harry. Have you seen him?" she asked breathlessly.

Chloe—who wasn't Eliza's aunt at all but merely the most respected woman amongst the slaves—shook her head and looked to the side at Uncle Tom. He smiled his slow, kind smile and wagged his head back and forth.

"Dat boy always be runnin' from you, Lizzie, 'til you stop

reactin'," he said gently. "You needn't worry. Saw him upstairs not five minutes ago. Look you in the library."

Eliza paused long enough to throw him a grateful smile, then turned and rushed up the stairs. When she threw the library door open, she saw Harry sneaking through the door to the master's parlor, his black curls shining in the morning light. She crouched down, keeping her footsteps soft, and crept after him toward the doorway.

When she got there, however, she stopped short at what she saw. Harry was talking to a very oddly-dressed man, and Shelby was not in the room. Looking the man up and down, she saw that he wore the most outrageous suit of clothes she'd ever seen—rose pink with yellow stripes, combined with a spotted tie and a ludicrous amount of lace. He'd pulled her Harry onto his lap and was looking at him with an acquisitive gleam in his eye.

Eliza gasped and rushed forward. "I'm so sorry to intrude, sir," she muttered. "I'll just take my son and get out of your way."

"Not at all, gal, he ain't doin' no harm," the man said, waving her away. "I'm Dan Haley, a friend of Shelby's. And what's your name?"

Eliza shut her mouth with a snap. She didn't like the look of the man and wanted to gather her son and go, but it seemed that he was inclined to talk. "Eliza, and that's Harry," she said grudgingly. "But we must go, sir, for we've our chores to see to."

"Now now, your boy here was just about to show me some of his tricks, and I've a mind to see them," the man said, his tone turning slightly darker. He turned on Harry then and shook him slightly. "Sing, boy. I want to see what you can do."

Harry, always quick to entertain, did just that. He began to sing a lovely song in a rich, clear voice that never should have belonged to such a young child. He jumped up and began dancing in time to the music, growing braver as the man clapped and laughed.

"Bravo!" said Haley, throwing Harry a penny. "What else can you do?"

The little boy took Haley's stick into his hand, humped his back up, and began hobbling around the room like a man with the rheumatism. His face was drawn into a mournful pucker, and he mimed spitting to the right and left, just as an old man would do. Eliza watched him closely. She'd seen him do it before, of course, and had always thought him a precocious little scamp.

However, she very much disliked the idea of him performing for this man. She liked even less the way the man was watching her son, as if he was a bug worth picking up.

Haley laughed and clapped. "More, boy! Give me more!"

At that moment Shelby walked through the parlor door, his eyes raking the room and coming to rest on Eliza. "Why Eliza," he said, surprised. "Whatever are you doing here? And with little Harry?" He glanced from one to the other, his eyes nervous, and Eliza paused, wondering. Why was the master reacting so badly?

"I've just come in for Harry, Mas'r, but this man won't let him go."

"The boy's performin' for me, Shelby, and I'd like to see what he does," the man said sharply.

"Well now, Haley, he has things to do around the house. Eliza, take the boy and go," Shelby muttered.

Relieved, Eliza darted forward, took Harry's hand, and pulled him toward the door. Once they were in the hall, she pushed Harry onward, whispering for him to go into the kitchen to see Aunt Chloe and get some sweets while she took care of some of her chores.

Rather than turning toward her own room, though, she ducked back against the door, listening closely to the master and his guest. There was something wrong with that man, and he'd had his hands all over her son, saying he wanted to know what the boy could do. She didn't know who he was, but she did want to know what he wanted with her son.

"That there gal's a beauty, Shelby. You could make a fortune off her," the man was saying.

Eliza gasped and covered her mouth. Sell her? Shelby would never!

"I don't need a fortune, Haley, and I would rather die than sell that girl. I'll thank you to keep a civil tongue in your head," Shelby snapped.

"Nonetheless, should you include her in our transaction, I'd be mighty pleased," Haley answered.

Eliza narrowed her eyes and ducked closer to the keyhole of the large oak door. Transaction? What transaction was he talking about?

"My wife would never allow it. She's raised that girl since she was a small child. Why, she thinks of her as a daughter."

"Well if you won't give me the girl, you'll give me her boy. Why, that boy can do impressions like none I've ever seen before—and that face! He's as gorgeous as the girl. He'll bring a pretty penny. I can turn him in a day! I know the very client—a man always in search of likely lookin' boys like that chap. Puts 'em to good use, if you know what I mean. Give me mother and son, I'll find a likely place for 'em both down New Orleans way."

Eliza gasped again. Why, he was talking about selling them! Turning her and Harry over to the man in the pink suit. She closed her eyes, willing herself away from this place, but her eyes flew open at the next line.

"I'd never take him from his mother, Haley, so don't ask it," Shelby answered, though Eliza thought she heard his voice quaking.

Suddenly, Mrs. Shelby was at her elbow, shaking her head. "Why Eliza, how many times have I told you not to go eavesdropping?" she asked. "Get to your chores right now, you naughty girl!"

So saying, she turned Eliza and smacked her smartly on the bottom, sending her off in a whirl of emotion and fear.

~

L ater that evening, Eliza held her son in her arms, wondering what on earth was going to happen to them. The man in pink had left the plantation earlier—she'd watched him ride away from one of the upstairs windows— and no one had said anything of him. But he'd asked the master to sell her—and Harry—and Shelby hadn't sent him directly from the house. She squeezed Harry tighter, making him squirm and complain. Surely Shelby would never sell her or Harry. He'd never sold any of his hands before, so why would he start now? And she'd been with them since she was a child. Why, they were more parents to her than master and mistress. Surely they wouldn't be able to sell her, not like some horse or piece of furniture.

Surely Shelby had told the man no and sent him away. Surely she was safe here, just as safe as she'd ever been. She rose and put Harry to bed, telling herself over and over again that they had a home here, and that nothing would happen to them.

CHAPTER 6

George stalked toward the front door of the main house on the Shelby plantation, guided by William, Harris' overseer. The man had insisted on coming with him —just as Harris had ordered—and hadn't stopped talking for the entire ride. That constant gloating, on top of Harris' outlandish statement that George should forget his marriage to Eliza and take Mina to his bed, had combined to create a burning fury in George's heart.

He schooled his features, hoping he didn't look as angry as he felt. This might be the last time he saw Eliza for some time, and he didn't want to frighten her or Harry with an angry countenance.

By the time the house slave opened the door to the Shelby home, he'd regained some control and shrugged his way out of William's clutches.

"Oliver," he said quietly, nodding to the house slave. "I'm here to see my wife."

He stepped over the threshold, ignoring William's muttered remarks about making it quick, and ducked into the darkness of the house. Aunt Chloe was bumping around in the kitchen, shouting out orders to her assistants, and from deeper in the house came laughter as some of the younger house slaves went about their chores. Despite himself, George felt his heart lift. Things had always been different in the Shelby house, as if it existed on a different plane altogether. Here, he'd always been treated as a man—not a beast. His wife had grown up here, practically a daughter to the master and mistress, and treated as a spoiled child.

The free and easy air of this place was one of the things he would miss most when he was gone.

He shook his head, putting aside his regrets, and pounded up the stairs, eager to see the most important residents of the house. He drew to a stop at the end of the first short hallway and knocked smartly on Eliza's door. She'd been given a suite adjacent to the master's and mistress' so that she would be within easy reach of Mrs. Shelby, and she took to her room every evening before dinner to spend time alone with Harry. George knew her habits and thought for certain that she'd be here.

Seconds later, she opened the door, her face brightening with recognition and then joy.

"Why George!" she exclaimed, throwing her arms around his neck. "What're you doin' here this late in the evenin'? I was wonderin' when you'd be back!"

George heaved a deep sigh, then pushed Eliza back into her room. Confused, she gestured toward their son, saying, "Harry's just come up to spend some time learnin' his letters. Look at how far he's come!" She gestured to the small chalkboard Mrs. Shelby had given their son, on which he was indeed practicing his letters. The boy looked up at his father and grinned, quite proud of himself.

"I wish he'd never been born!" George muttered, tears in his eyes. He threw himself into one of the two chairs in the room and looked morosely around the place. It was well decorated and roomy enough, but did that replace the freedom they should have? "I wish I'd never been born and that you'd never met me!"

Eliza frowned. "Why George, what do you mean? How could you wish such a thing?" she asked quietly.

"Oh Eliza, Eliza, you're the most beautiful woman I've ever seen, and you have the best heart I've had the good fortune to know. I wish you'd never heard of me. I'll drag you down —I know it—and you deserve better!" He lowered his face into his hands, his heart breaking at what he knew he must do.

At this, Eliza's eyes filled with tears, her face falling with disappointment, and he took her quickly into his arms. "*Sh, sh*, my love, I don't mean to hurt you," he whispered gently. "It's just that my heart is broken, and I fear I'll break yours as well."

"George, I don't understand. What's made you so angry?"

He sat back and held Eliza out at arm's length, looking deeply into her eyes. "Eliza, things have gone badly for me—so badly!—and I don't know what I'll do. Harris forced me back onto the plantation, and since my return, it's been nothin' but the most terrible work! He even drowned Carlo!"

"No, not Carlo!" Eliza said, horrified.

"Yes, he allowed his son to murder my little friend, and he's gone out of his way to force me down." His voice broke on the last word, and he paused for a moment, trying to collect his emotions. The news he was going to give her was bad enough. His tears would just make it worse.

"I'm leavin', my love, and you must promise me that you'll wait for me to return."

"What?" she snapped, the color draining from her face.

Harry, realizing that his parents were at odds, stumbled toward his mother and took her hand, looking up at George with wide, serious eyes. "Papa, why are you angry?" he asked, his voice full of childish innocence. "Why is Mamma cryin'?"

George took his son up into his lap as well so that he had Harry on one knee and Eliza on the other. "I must leave, Eliza, for I can stand it here no longer. Harris has abused me greatly, with more disrespect than he's ever shown before, and I can't stand it anymore. Who is he to judge me? Who is he to take me from my job and tell me to do something else? Or tell me that I must marry another woman? What's given him the right?" With every word, his anger grew until he was nearly shouting in frustration. He dropped back against the chair, his chest heaving, and swallowed heavily.

"George, George!" Eliza said, falling to her knees in front of him. "I knew he'd taken you from the factory, but...marry another woman? Whatever do you mean? I'm your wife already!"

"He says we can't be married anymore, my dear, and that I must take one of his house slaves to my bed, to make babies for him. It's too, too bad, Eliza, and I won't do it. I'll die before I do!"

"But George, how can he? We were married here, in front of a pastor! In front of God!"

"Harris cares about God as much as God cares about us slaves."

"George, don't say such things. God will deliver us from these hardships."

"I have no plans to wait for His deliverance. I'm going soon, to Canada, and you must wait for me to come for you." He stood and grasped her hands, pulling her to her feet in his passion. "I'll live there as a free man, and when I have the money, I'll come and take you—and young Harry—away with me."

"To Canada?" Eliza asked, seemingly overwhelmed. "And leave here, leave Mas'r and Missis? I could never!"

"Eliza, you're not safe here, just as no slave is safe! You can never tell when they're going to alter your life, or sell you away. When I return, you must go with me!"

"But George—"

"I'll hear no more about it," George said, putting a finger to her lips. "This is my path, this has always been my path, and you know I've meant to leave for some time now."

"You've always wanted to leave. I just never thought you'd

actually do it. What if you're taken...?" She let her words fade away at the thought and looked up at him, pleading for him to think rationally.

"I'll die before I'm taken, Eliza, and that's a fact," he answered firmly, knowing in his heart that neither of those things would ever happen. "And so good-bye, my love, for now. I leave for Canada within the week, but I swear I'll be back for you within the year. Remember me in your prayers and remind Harry often that he has a father who loves him."

Then, with the sharp, jerky actions of a man who hates what he has to do, he ducked down to quickly kiss her lips and Harry's forehead and then sped from the room. His heart broke as he closed the door behind him, for he didn't know when he would see them again, though he'd promised that he'd be back for them. He had no idea how he was going to do any of it—get away from the Harris plantation or make his way to Canada—and he wasn't sure what he would do when he got there or how he was going to return for his wife and son.

But he knew that he had to do so. His heart told him, without any doubt, that this was the only way. Harris had taken everything of value here, and George would not submit to it any longer.

CHAPTER 7

The night had grown dark and cold by the time George returned to the Harris plantation. He had been pushed and shoved along for the entire journey by William, who had become enraged at how long George took with Eliza. George, who despised William almost as much as he despised Harris, had held his tongue the entire way home, though William had run his own mouth mercilessly.

After all, if he was going to leave, he needed to keep his head down and avoid attention and trouble until he left. If they were watching him too closely, he'd never get away.

When they arrived back at the men's slave quarters, which were dark and dingy and badly in need of repair and washing, he was shocked to see Harris himself standing in the doorway, a smirk on his face.

"This won't be your home no more, boy," the master

sneered. "I already told you you're to marry Mina. You're movin.'"

George stared at the man, speechless. *Already?* He'd barely found out about this new scheme, and Harris already expected him to begin this new work? He'd hoped for a couple of days, at least. "But sir, surely—"

"I said now, boy! Don't give me your lip!" Harris snarled. William pushed George from behind, adding muscle to Harris' words, and George stumbled.

"Sir, I thought I'd spend this last night on my pallet, at least. Get accustomed to the idea of a new wife," he said quietly, reminding himself that he meant to pretend obedience, at least for now.

"You thought wrong, boy, now get your things," William muttered, shoving George again.

Harris' hand shot out to catch George, though, and he forced George's chin up to look him in the eye. "You tell that Shelby gal things was done, way I told you?" he asked sharply. George refused to answer, fighting to hold his tongue against all the things he wanted to say to this man, and Harris, taking George's silence as a yes, nodded once. "Well then, ain't nothin' stoppin' you from beddin' Mina, and you'll start tonight," he said, as though the situation warranted nothing more than his approval.

Suddenly George's anger overwhelmed his self-control and he snarled, snapping his teeth at the master. "Eliza is my wife, Harris, and there isn't anything you can say to change that!" he shouted. "You might be able to keep me away from her, but you can never force me to take another woman to my bed!"

Harris laughed, enraging George still further, and took two steps back. "Well boy, that's where you're wrong. Truth is, I can make you do whatever I want. Seems you just need some remindin'." His eyes traveled behind George to William, and he nodded once. "Bring him."

Without another word, Harris pushed past George and strode away. George turned to watch him go, his mind racing. What had the man meant by that? He could never force George to bed another woman, never! Why, it would be—

Before he could complete the thought, William had grabbed him by the arm and shoved him forward again. "Looks like it's the whippin' tree for you 'gain, boy," he muttered. "Should know better than to question your master by now. I thought they said you were smart?" He laughed a loud, cruel laugh, and George's heart sank.

The whipping tree. He knew it well, of course, and had found himself tied to it many times before. Tall, it was, and long-since dead, with gnarled branches and roots that stuck up out of the ground, still well suited for tying hands up and legs out to the side. And to receive that punishment for refusing to bed another woman...

His heart hardened at the thought. Harris had no right—no right to tell George how to work or who to take to his bed! And no right to punish him for wanting a say in his own life. What sort of country was this, that would award that sort of power to one man and not another? What sort of laws would allow this sort of abuse?

By the time they got to the tree, he'd decided once and for all that this would be the end of it. He'd taken all he could take, and he wasn't going to take any more.

He would run—tonight—if he was still capable of walking.

"You preparin' your soul, boy?" Harris snarled from the side of the tree where he was stoking the fire. Then he turned to another of the slaves. "Fetch me my whip! Warm my brandin' iron!" he screamed, his voice filled with excitement.

George glared at the man, his heart brimming with hatred, and considered all the things he would do to him if—when —he got the chance. He couldn't answer, though, for he was already pressed face-first against the tree, his arms yanked above him, the fire glinting in his peripheral vision. Behind him, he could hear the murmur of the slaves called to witness the punishment, along with Harris' voice calling out to the others in the darkness.

"Secure him tightly, William. I don't want him squirmin' away!" the man shouted, laughing. "Ben! Bring me that whip. The new one! Should be stiff enough to do a creditable job."

George pushed his forehead against the tree in front of him and groaned. *No matter how much it hurts, you will not give in,* he told himself firmly. *You will stand strong and defend your wife and child! You're standing up for your rights as a man, and there's nothing more important than that. Not pain, not abuse—*

Then the first blow fell, and then the second, the cat-o'-nine-tails whistling through the cold night air. A moment later, his knees gave out. The pain was worse than he'd remembered, each blow falling heavier than the last, finding skin that was overly sensitive in the brutal cold of the night. Before long, the skin on his back was bruising and then tearing open. Another strike, and then another. He could hear Harris laughing, though the murmuring of the slaves had fallen silent.

George cried out at the next blow, unable to stop himself. "Eliza!" he cried, wishing desperately for her warm, loving embrace.

"No!" Harris roared. The blows began to fall harder and faster, and George screamed. He was more of a man than Harris, and he could beat this man, he thought desperately. He would hold true to his word, and to his wife.

"Eliza!" he shouted defiantly, knowing that it would drive Harris to the brink of madness. "Eliza is my wife!"

The next blow knocked his feet from under him, blood running down his back and legs. He gasped, struggling with the pain. *Eliza*, he told himself, pulling her face to the front of his mind and trying to focus on it. She would save him. The thought of her love would save him.

But the next blow fell on his raw, bleeding skin with twice as much strength, and tears began to flow down his face. The man was going to kill him, he realized. He was going to use this whipping as an excuse to rid himself of a trouble-some slave, and no one would ever judge him for it. He would receive no punishment. George would be gone, and Harris would go unpunished and do the same to others, given half a chance.

The only way George would survive to see his wife and son again—the only way Harris would be brought to justice—was if George gave in.

"You and your kin have been nothin' but trouble, ever since I bought you," Harris said breathlessly. "Your wench of a mother dirtied my clothin' with her grovelin'. Your sister refused my wishes until I had to sell her down the river to get rid of her. And now you—" He paused to land one more blow. "You insist on your little rebellions. Well, I'll show you who's boss, boy. Who's your wife now? Tell me! Tell me!"

"Mina," George whispered, knowing that this would be his only escape.

"Louder!"

"Mina!" he shouted, praying that Eliza would forgive him.

Suddenly the blows stopped, and he sagged lifelessly in relief. A moment later, though, he felt his hand pulled down from the ropes and saw Harris' sly eyes to his left.

"What—" he began.

A second later, the glowing branding iron was pressed into his right palm, searing its mark into the skin there. He screamed and dropped to his knees, jerking against the agonizing heat, but William held him down from above while Harris pressed the iron deeper into his skin. The edges of his vision began to fade from the pain, though he could hardly think to notice it. The pain was worse than anything he'd ever felt in his life.

Finally, the brand was pulled away, leaving behind the scent

CARL WATERS & DR. KAL CHINYERE

of scorched meat, and George cradled his hand against his chest.

"That's to remind you where you belong, boy, and who you belong to" Harris said, leaning down to whisper into his ear. "Now get to Mina's room and let your new wife doctor you, the way she should."

CHAPTER 8

Eliza sat in her room, still trying to understand what her husband had said to her. He had left hours earlier, but she hadn't found the strength to stand up again, no matter how much Harry fussed about his hunger. She couldn't believe he was leaving—actually leaving, not just talking about it, the way he had so many times before. He was in a bad situation—that much was obvious—and she couldn't say she was surprised. Harris had always disliked her husband for the way he carried himself, and it had only gotten worse since George had gone to the hemp factory. George had certainly told her about it more than once. He'd had more access to books there and had sought to educate himself as much as possible, with Wilson's blessing.

And every book he read just made him more hateful to Harris.

George had always meant to leave, of course, and had thought the education would help him. But now that it came down to it…

"I never thought he actually would," she concluded quietly.

"Would what, Mamma?" Harry asked anxiously, hanging off her knees and watching her with serious, thoughtful eyes.

"Would leave us, child," she answered, gathering him into her arms. "Your father's gone on…on a journey, and I don't know whether he's comin' back. I just never believed it would actually happen."

"And we'll go with him," Harry concluded quickly, pulling away from her and moving toward the other side of the room, as if he was going to start packing his things immediately.

Eliza laughed, shook her head at her son, but then paused, thinking. After all, that was what George had said—that he meant for them to go to Canada with him. Not now, of course. He'd said he would come back for them. He'd said that he didn't think they were safe here, that anything might happen as long as they belonged to someone else.

This brought her mind firmly back to the problem at hand. George was in a bad situation, that much was obvious, but she couldn't afford to forget the things going on in her own home. That man in the room with Shelby had been a trader —she was sure of it—and he'd been too interested in her son for her liking. She choked at the thought.

Harry came rushing back, as if he'd heard her soft sob and thoughts, and reached up to hug her. "What's wrong now, Mamma?" he asked gently.

"Only that I think we're in trouble, child, for that man you talked to earlier is a bad man, and I don't know what he means to do." Her thoughts flew back to the way the man had dandled Harry on his knee, bragging to Shelby about the friends who dealt in such boys. She didn't think Shelby would sell her or Harry—she was certain that Mrs. Shelby would never allow it—but what if she was wrong?

What if Shelby did mean to sell her son, and to that terrible man, who would pass him on to anyone he wanted?

She would never know, she realized, until it was too late. She needed to find out what Shelby meant to do so that she could decide what she was going to do herself. The master and mistress always discussed their days before they went to bed, she knew. And there was a large closet between her room and theirs—a shared wall, in fact.

It was the perfect place to hide. And she needed to hear that conversation.

She glanced at the one window in her room—the one that led out onto the verandah—and saw that the sky had turned a deep, dusky purple. Shadows were crawling up from the ground, getting ready to meet the night sky. Her own room was dark since she had yet to light her candles. She looked at the clock and realized that her master and mistress would be in their room now, or nearly there. As Mrs. Shelby's maid, that meant she had work to do. She put Harry to bed, murmuring to him that he must go to sleep like a good boy now, and quickly, for she might have need of him later. She paused to sing to him for a moment, murmuring out his favorite lullaby in her softest voice. Once his heavy eyes closed, she rose and hurried from the room.

When she arrived in the master bedroom, she found Mrs. Shelby already dressed in her nightgown and sitting in front of her mirror.

"Why child, why didn't you or Harry come for dinner? And why are you just arriving to help me prepare for bed?" Mrs. Shelby asked, half scolding her. "I've been here for thirty minutes at least, waiting for you."

"Harry is feelin' ill, Missis, and I had to sit with him for longer than usual," Eliza lied, not wanting to tell her mistress the truth—that she'd been in her room, worried sick over what might happen to her husband and son.

"Well, boy's had an exciting day, no doubt. I heard tell we had a visitor."

Eliza, seeing her opening, decided that this was the best chance she was going to have. "Yes ma'am, and in fact..." Suddenly she fell at Mrs. Shelby's feet, unable to restrain herself, and laid her head in the woman's lap. "There was a man here, and he talked about buyin' me or my Harry, and though Mas'r Shelby told him that he wouldn't hear of it, I'm so frightened, ma'am! Surely Mas'r wouldn't sell us, either of us, to that man!"

Mrs. Shelby snorted at that and put her hands on Eliza's head. "Now child, what could you be thinking? 'Course Mr. Shelby wouldn't sell the two of you! Why, I'd never hear of it, not one bit! You're like family to us."

"But that man said—" Eliza sobbed.

"That man didn't have any right to say anything, and you're worrying about something that you don't need to think on," Mrs. Shelby interrupted, lifting Eliza's chin firmly.

Eliza searched the other woman's eyes, desperately wanting to believe her, and saw that Mrs. Shelby was telling her the truth, so far as she knew it. "You won't let him sell my Harry, will you?" she whispered.

"No, child. Now get up and brush my hair so that I might

get to bed. Mr. Shelby will be here soon, and I have certain things I need to say to him."

Eliza rose as she was told and moved behind Mrs. Shelby to brush out her long, graying curls. The job was a quick one, for she'd brushed the woman's hair earlier in the day, and within minutes she was back out in the hallway, drying her eyes and moving quickly toward the closet between her room and the master bedroom.

Mrs. Shelby had said that nothing would come of that man's visit, but Eliza would never feel sure until she heard it for herself, from Shelby's own mouth.

She'd barely entered the closet and put her ear to the space between the door and the jamb when she heard Shelby himself enter the room.

"Why, Emily, already in bed?" he said jovially. "I thought I might read for a bit."

"Before you do, Arthur, I've something to ask you," Mrs. Shelby said quietly. Eliza's heart pounded, for she knew exactly what her mistress was going to ask, and though she wanted to know the answer, she was frightened of what that answer might be. Still, she pressed harder against the door so that she wouldn't miss anything.

"Who was that low-bred fellow you had here today?" Mrs. Shelby asked.

Eliza heard a long, uncomfortable pause, and for a moment she thought Shelby wasn't going to answer at all. Then: "It's best that you don't concern yourself with him. He's nothing to do with you, and I'd rather you don't have any doings with that man."

"Who is he, Arthur?" Mrs. Shelby—never one to be put off, Eliza thought—asked sharply.

"His name is Dan Haley. He's a trader, Emily, though it pains me to say it, and he came on business."

"What business could he possibly have here? Why, I could never believe that you would allow such a person into our home! Eliza told me the man was trying to buy her Harry, but I said—"

"He was—is—trying to buy the both of them, if you want to know the truth," Shelby said, his voice tired. "And Tom as well."

Eliza bit her tongue sharply to keep from crying out. It was just as she'd suspected then, and even worse, if Shelby was talking to Mrs. Shelby about it.

Mrs. Shelby, evidently just as surprised as Eliza, took her time answering. "What?" she asked finally. "How could you even entertain such a notion? These folks are like our children! Why, I've raised them as our own, taught them to read and mind their manners, tended their wounds when they're hurt... How could you think of selling any of them, Arthur? How?"

Eliza nodded in silent agreement, her hand over her mouth to keep her cries of horror stifled.

"Emily, you don't know the situation," Shelby answered quietly. "The plantation fell onto some hard times recently. You remember the trouble we had last year, and the neighboring plantation owners refusing to extend us any credit. Well, Haley loaned me the money I needed. He owns several bills of credit on the plantation, and well, to be frank, he won't settle for money a'tall. Fact is, he wants Tom and Eliza or Tom and Harry in payment and won't hear of anything else. I'm in a corner, don't you see?"

"But Arthur—"

"Emily, what would you have me do? I've already told him that you would never hear of me sending Eliza away, but if I don't give him Tom and Harry, he might take the whole plantation. Then we would all be homeless. What you must ask yourself is whether it's better to let go of two so that we might keep the rest safe."

There was no response from the mistress then, and Eliza

closed her eyes in fear. Surely Mrs. Shelby wouldn't let him do this? Surely, surely she'd stop him. Why, to send her Harry away—and Uncle Tom too!—with a man they didn't know and to an unknown future...

"Well, when you put it that way, I do see your point, Arthur," the woman finally answered, her voice defeated. "I can't stand it—I really can't—but I don't see that there's anything to be done, is there?"

"No, Emily, there's not," he said. "Haley's coming in the morning for the two of them, and nothing to be done for it. Now let me come to bed so that we might sleep, and perhaps dream of a world where this isn't the case."

At that, Eliza backed quickly away from the door. Shelby might come into the closet for his night things, and she couldn't be caught there. She turned to her own rooms, her mind spinning at what she'd heard, and stumbled toward Harry's bed. He was sleeping peacefully, the dear boy, and she reached out to touch his flushed cheek. Her son—sold? To travel down the river? No! She wouldn't think of what they'd do with him. The possibilities were too terrible. Part of her mind refused to believe it at all. How could it be? After she'd trusted the master and mistress with her very life, and that of her son!

She'd have to hide him, she realized suddenly. Haley was

coming in the morning to collect him. They'd send her to another room—or perhaps on an errand to get her out of the way—and when she returned, her son would be gone, with nothing left and no word of explanation. She'd heard stories of it being done before on other plantations. Well, she didn't mean for Harry to be here when Haley returned. She would tidy him away, take him someplace where the trader would never find him, and save him from the life the trader had threatened.

"Run to Canada," she said quietly. Yes, it was the only way. George was going already, wasn't he? She had thought him crazy, but now ... now she could see that it was the only choice she had.

CHAPTER 9

In his dream, George was running from the fire. It licked at his feet and legs, burning him again and again, and flew along the ground faster than he could run. Ahead of him, he knew that Eliza and Harry waited. He had to get to them before the fire did. If he reached them, they would all escape. But, if the fire beat him…

He screamed at the thought and shot up from the pallet, breathing heavily, his eyes running over the room, trying to find the ones he'd been dreaming about.

A dream, he realized. Just a dream. Eliza and Harry weren't here at all. He scowled at the thought, trying to remember where he was. The room was in the slave quarters—dark and squalid with no furniture and only a pot for pissing in. But it wasn't his. It was Mina's, he realized. Then it came back to him—the order to marry Mina and the trip to see Eliza. Harris waiting for him when he got back. The fight. The beating.

The brand.

He glanced down at his hand and saw a new wound in the shape of an "H" there. It hadn't begun to scab yet, but it looked healthier than he expected, as if someone had cleaned it.

"Only with water," a strange voice said, and he looked up, surprised.

Mina sat on the pallet next to him, her eyes large and dark, and a soft rag in her hand. He opened his mouth and shut it again, confused.

"They brought you here when you passed out," she said quietly. "Said this was your rightful place now. I've been cleanin' your back and your hand, tryin' to get the dirt out. Didn't mean to wake you, though."

George shifted suddenly, remembering, and his back twinged. Ouch. Yes, the beating. He'd be sore for days. But there were other things to discuss—things far more important than his back. "I ... Mina, you know that I cannot—"

"I know very well that you've got a family," she answered

quickly, pulling his hand back into her lap to continue cleaning it.

His heart clenched at her tone, and he paused for a moment. He'd known Mina for many years and had counted her a friend in his time on the plantation. She was a beautiful woman—dark skinned with large, soft features—and had a heart that gave itself easily to others. She'd also been a particular friend of his sister, Charlotte, before Harris sold her down the river.

In another time and another place, she would have made a wonderful wife and a loyal ally. The last thing he wanted to do was hurt her.

"I cannot marry you," he said gently. "I'm a happily married man already, and there isn't anything I would do to change that. It has nothing to do with you."

"I know," she answered. "I don't want this either, but what can I do? Harris has told me that I must bed you, and he's a way of gettin' what he wants. Ain't the first time he's forced me to do somethin' I don't want to do, after all." Her voice drifted off, and George remembered the rumors he'd heard —that Harris had taken Mina to his bed, forcing her to pleasure him every night, despite her wishes.

"You know he tried to do the same thing to my sister Charlotte. You saw it with your own eyes. And she never gave in to him."

"And he sold her down the river for her pains," Mina remembered, smiling wryly. "You suggestin' she's better off now, and that I should do the same?"

"Don't rightly know," George said sadly. "I haven't seen her since she left."

"Exactly," Mina answered. "Just the same life in a different place, and I don't think it's any better there than it is here."

At that, George reached out and grabbed her arm. "It has to be better somewhere else. I can't stay here—I just can't. Harris is goin' to kill me or drive me out of my mind. I know I'd be better off somewhere else."

Mina frowned. "If you stay, I'll be a good wife to you. I'll help you through."

He laughed. "No amount of help is goin' to keep me safe here. He means to kill me, don't you see? Besides, I'll never love any woman but Eliza," he finished. "I must leave and find my life elsewhere."

"But where will you go?" Mina asked, her eyes beginning to grow curious.

George noticed the curiosity and saw his chance. He leaned

forward, eager to talk about his plans. "To Canada," he whispered. "Where I can be free. I'll travel at night, follow the North Star until I get there. Then I'll start a new life. Be my own man."

Mina gasped. "But, you'd never make it. Harris has patrollers, dogs, slave catchers... You'll be caught—or worse, killed. You know the laws 'bout slaves runnin'. It don't matter if they're dead or alive when they come back."

"I'll die if I stay here. If I leave, at least I have the chance to live—or die—as a free man."

Mina sighed and gave him a long, hard look. Finally she relented, her lips turning up in a slight smile. "Well, I can see that you're set on it, and I've known you long enough to know that once you make up your mind, it ain't possible to talk you out of it."

"So you'll help me?" he asked hopefully.

She nodded firmly. "If anyone can make it, it's you. You're smart enough, and I know you're brave enough. I'll help you in any way I can, but..."

"But what?" he asked quickly. Anything, he'd promise anything, if it meant he could count her as an ally.

She pushed her lips out in thought, then nodded once at her mental conversation, and looked up at him. "You must promise that you'll come back for me, George. I won't stay here either, not if I know there's another way to live."

George squeezed her arm in agreement, nodding as well. "I'm leaving Saturday night. As long as I make it, I will be back for you. That's a promise."

CHAPTER 10

Eliza slipped out onto the verandah of her room, glancing around the front lawn to see if anyone else was around. It was nearly ten o'clock, and she didn't expect any of the slaves to be about, but she needed to be sure. Below her, she saw that the lawn and driveway were as dark as could be, the barn just a faint shape in the distance. On the other side of the house, she knew, the slaves would be asleep in their quarters, their fires burning low for the night. It was very cold out and no one would be out if they could help it. She'd waited until Mr. and Mrs. Shelby had fallen asleep and then roused Harry from his bed, dressing him quickly in some of his warmest clothes and slipping on his jacket. She herself wore two of her dresses, one on top of another, and had some of their belongings and a small amount of chicken and biscuits, plus several apples, tied into a small pack and strapped to her back.

It wasn't much food, but it would have to keep them for the night, at least. She didn't mean to come back.

Before she left the room, she'd written a very short note to Mrs. Shelby, telling her that she loved her dearly and thought of her as a mother, but she couldn't stay there when her son was in trouble. She only hoped the mistress would believe her and remember her fondly.

She slipped down the steps to the ground below, clutching Harry tightly to her. He was barely awake, poor chap, and confused as anything, but she didn't see any way around it. She needed to get to Uncle Tom's cabin first and warn him about what she'd heard, then she'd run to George. With luck, Uncle Tom would choose to come with her and save himself. With more luck, they'd reach George before he left himself. The road to Canada was going to be dangerous, but with two men at her side, she thought they'd be safe enough.

She darted across the porch, praying that Aunt Chloe hadn't put out the kitchen fires and gone to bed, and stopped, startled, when she saw a large, black shadow on the porch.

"Who's there?" she gasped. "Who is that?"

A low huff answered her, and she laughed gently. Why, it was no one more dangerous than Bruno, the old Newfoundland in charge of guarding the house.

"Bruno," she scolded. "You nearly scared me to death!"

The dog walked over, unapologetic for this lapse in manners, and sniffed at her hands and then at Harry's feet. He looked up, seemingly ready for the adventure, and Eliza shrugged.

"Well, I'm only goin' to Uncle Tom's cabin after all, so you might as well come that far." She set off toward the slave quarters, the dog at her heels and Harry tucked firmly into her arms.

When she reached the cabin, the lights were still on. That was a relief—it meant she didn't need to get Uncle Tom and Aunt Chloe up from their bed. The news was going to be bad enough, she thought, without the additional complication of waking the couple. She glanced in the window to see Chloe and Tom both in the kitchen area, washing what passed for their dishes. Their two sons and young daughter were already asleep on their pallets, three fuzzy heads lined up in a row.

Unwilling to waste any time, she tapped firmly on the window to get their attention and gestured toward the door. Aunt Chloe turned in surprise, one hand on her heart, and opened her mouth into an "O" at the sight of Eliza. Uncle Tom—reacting rather more rationally—headed directly for the door and threw it open.

"Why Eliza," he muttered. "You scared the wits out of us! What're you doin' out and about at this time o' night, girl? And dressed as if you're travelin'. What's amiss?"

"Oh Uncle Tom," Eliza said, rushing past him into the house. "It's been the most awful day, and I have terrible news. I'm leavin' tonight, for I can't stay here anymore, and you must come with me."

She went on to tell him about Haley's visit to Shelby, what she'd overheard of their conversation, and what Mr. Shelby had told Mrs. Shelby, her heart jumping up in her throat. With each sentence, Tom's face grew more and more despondent.

"So you see," she finally finished, "I must go, to save poor Harry, and you must come with me, Uncle Tom. That trader'll be back in the mornin' to take you away, and who knows what will become of you?"

Aunt Chloe looked from Eliza back to Uncle Tom, her face a mask of shock and disbelief. She stepped forward to take her husband's hand. "Tom, she's right. You've got to go. Can't stay here to let that man take you away." She turned toward Eliza, all business. "And where will you go, child? Do you have a plan?"

Eliza nodded firmly. "I'll go to the Harris plantation tonight, to find George. He's leavin' anyhow, and I can't see any reason for us to travel apart. Uncle Tom might come with us, to make his way to Canada."

Aunt Chloe turned back toward her husband, her eyes torn between hope and terror. "See there, Tom, Eliza's got a plan all set, and you must go with her. I don't see any way 'round it, not if you're to be safe. We'll be here waitin', case you ever come back for us, but for now you've got to think of yourself."

But Uncle Tom, who was born a slave on the Shelby plantation and had been raised up to be the plantation's foreman, gave a slow, gentle shake of his head. "You can't go to the Harris place, Eliza. That man pays too well for runaways. That area is always crawlin' with patrollers at night, and you'll be caught." He turned sorrowfully toward his wife and took her hands in his. "Chloe, don't you see I must stay? Eliza says that trader's got the papers to the plantation. Means Mas'r Shelby has to give him someone or lose all. Pains me to leave you, but if he's got to sell anyone, it's his choice to sell me."

"But your papers!" Chloe gasped. "Tom, Mas'r Shelby promised you your freedom—this very summer!" She let out a sob and grabbed for him, pressing her face into his chest. "Who knows where you'll be sent? We'll never see you again!"

CARL WATERS & DR. KAL CHINYERE

He put her gently from him, a single tear running down his cheek. "Better me go than all of you," he answered. "If Mas'r doesn't sell me, the trader will likely take the plantation itself. Then he'll take all of you. Sell you the way he'd sell me, send you all out into the world. Least this way I know you'll be here, safe."

Eliza watched, her heart breaking, but then she shook herself. Uncle Tom had made up his mind, and she didn't understand it, but she didn't have time to stand around waiting for him to decide otherwise.

"Well then, I must be on my own way," she muttered firmly. "Uncle Tom, you're certain you won't come with me?" At a shake of his head, she nodded and stepped back toward the door. "Then I pray you'll take care of yourself and that the Lord will watch over you. For myself and my son, we're for Canada. And I hope you'll pray for us too."

"Follow the North Star, Eliza, if you must go," Uncle Tom told her quickly. "Up Ohio way. I expect you've brought your travelin' papers?" He waited for her nod, then continued. "Use those papers to catch a ferry across the river. Then you'll be on your way. But you mustn't go to the Harris plantation. Never fear, I'll get word to George that you've left. I trust he'll find you his own self."

Eliza nodded again and paused to kiss Uncle Tom on the

cheek. "Please take care of yourself," she murmured. Then she stepped through the door, shutting it firmly behind her, and made her way into the dark, already deciding on which route to take. Uncle Tom said it was too dangerous to stop for George, and she believed him. Harris had always been overly reactive about things like slaves running away, and she'd heard tell that he went out of his way to guard his property.

No, she couldn't go there. And that meant they would be on the road by themselves. The sooner they got to Ohio, she decided, the safer they'd be.

CHAPTER 11

S he'd been traveling for what felt like hours and hadn't seen any light since leaving Uncle Tom's cabin. Though she'd been scared of the dark as a young girl, Eliza now found that the darkness had sharpened her other senses, until she felt she could hear almost anything. This was, however, both a blessing and a curse as every sound terrified her. She was startled by yet another sound at that moment, this time from her left, and she shuddered with nerves. She wasn't used to being in the woods at night and had never realized what it was like to be out here in the dark. The woods were both terrifyingly quiet and loud at the same time, and she jumped at every sound, positive that someone had sent the slave catchers after her.

Another branch snapped behind her, the dried wood cracking like a gunshot in the moonlight, and Eliza was spooked, sprinting for several feet with Harry pressed tightly against her chest. She knew the Shelbys were sleeping—it was, after all, the middle of the night—and even if they had woken, they certainly wouldn't have sent any catchers after her. But the patrollers roamed this part of the country on their own and didn't often wait for a plantation owner to call them.

The Shelbys might not have sent them, but there were slave catchers everywhere, and if they found her, it would all be finished. For both her and Harry.

She peered deeply into the forest, looking for any sign of life, but saw only more dense foliage, the bushes peppering the ground around the trees, making it impossible to see farther than ten feet ahead of her. An owl hooted to her left, the noise echoing eerily through the branches, and she jerked. Were there wolves out here as well? Bears? Something worse?

"The Lord is my shepherd, I shall not want," she murmured, deciding to take comfort in her favorite psalm. If God was on her side, after all, the slave catchers would miss her entirely and she'd find her way safely to Ohio. "He maketh me to lie down in green pastures: He leadeth me beside the still waters."

She shifted Harry in her arms, pausing in her recital for a moment. The boy was sound asleep, thank the good Lord; it meant that he was through with worrying, at least for now. And though he was a firm, solid lad and should have been heavy for her slight frame, she'd found that she could carry him easily, despite the difficult going and lack of light.

It hadn't been so easy when they first left Uncle Tom's cabin. Harry had asked her time and again where they were going, and why, and when they would meet George, and why they hadn't brought a torch with them so they could see where they were going, or a blanket on which they could sit when they were tired.

In short, he'd thought of all the things that would have made the journey more comfortable. Of course, those things had all been impossible.

"We have to go quietly," she'd hushed him. "No one else knows that we're leaving, so we have to go by ourselves, and without light, and even without your father."

"But why, Ma?" he'd asked again.

"Because a bad man was coming to take you away, Harry, and I'm protecting you," she finally said. That had put an end to his questioning, being both threatening and decisive, and he'd fallen asleep soon after, much to Eliza's relief.

"He maketh me lie down in green pastures: He leadeth me beside the still waters," she whispered, continuing her psalm. Although she knew she shouldn't be speaking out loud, she couldn't seem to help herself; the sound of her own voice drowned out the sounds of the forest and made her feel safer. Not so alone.

"He restoreth my soul: He leadeth me in the path of right-eousness for His name's sake." She stopped for a moment to focus on her breathing; they'd hit a slope now, and it was more difficult for her to make her way up. Wearing two dresses had been both a blessing and a curse. The extra material was keeping her warm but made traveling much more difficult, thanks to its bulk. Still, she was glad of the additional layer between her skin and the sharp, cold night air.

Besides, when they got to Canada, she would need the extra dress. She was certain of it, for the idea of failure had come and gone by this time. There were sounds in the forest, yes, but they weren't the slave catchers. They weren't the dogs. The Lord was watching over her, and He was going to help her get her son to safety. He wouldn't let them fail. For the first time, she started to believe what George was always talking about—that men deserved to be free and to live their own lives.

For the first time, she thought that God might be of the same opinion as George. And if that was true, her faith in

Him would lead her to the Promised Land. It would save her son.

"Yea, though I walk through the valley of the shadow of death, I will fear no evil: for Thou art with me; Thy rod and Thy staff they comfort me. Thou preparest a table before me in the presences of mine enemies," she said, thinking of Haley and the fact that he would never lay hands on her son. Her voice grew in volume then, despite her wishes to keep quiet, and the words began to match the steps of her feet.

"Thou anointest my head with oil; my cup runneth over. Surely goodness and mercy shall follow me all the days of my life: and I will dwell in the house of the Lord forever."

She came to the end of the psalm, stomping heavily on the last three words, and smiled gently to herself, victorious in her heart. Yes, the Lord would watch over them as they traveled. And they would make their way to Canada, where she would find George and start their life anew.

CHAPTER 12

George glanced up at the horse in front of him, wondering if the horses would miss him at all. He'd been tending them for only a few weeks now, but he thought they'd grown accustomed to each other, maybe even learning to like each other. He'd always felt an affinity to animals like this—dogs, horses, even the occasional cat. They had a way of loving others without any judgment, he thought—of giving any man or woman equal chance at affection, without regard to race or status.

If only humanity itself could be that way.

The barn around them echoed with the soft sounds of the horses making their beds or chewing solidly on the end of their morning meal. The building rose up around him, scented with the familiar, oat smell of the stable, and George relaxed for a moment, at ease with the animals.

Then William cleared his throat at George's pause, and George set to work again, reaching under the horse to pull the girth tight. His back—still fresh and raw from the whipping—twinged painfully, and he grunted in pain, wondering if he'd torn open the wounds again. Mina had done her best to clean the marks, but they still hadn't begun to scab, and any decent man would have given him time to recover.

Of course, no one had ever said that Harris or William were decent men. George's eyes narrowed at the thought, and he pursed his lips. Devils, the both of them, and he couldn't get away from here quickly enough.

Then a new thought came to him: Mina was working on getting his supplies together right now so that he'd be ready to escape in a few nights. These were his last days as a slave, come hell or high water.

He rose to see that William had left him alone and sighed in relief. The man got under his skin, and no mistake. He was just about to move to another horse when he heard a whisper from the shadows.

"Mista George," a young voice said.

Frowning, George walked toward the corner and then out of the stable and around to the back, looking for the owner of the voice. He paused to glance behind a tree, and there he saw Pete, Uncle Tom's son, from the Shelby plantation.

"Pete, what're you doin' here?" George asked, rushing toward the boy and taking him by the shoulder. He glanced around, concerned. "You know Harris doesn't take kindly to visitors. You'll be in trouble if you're seen."

Pete nodded. "I know, Mista George, but Pa sent me. Told me I had to run and find you, right quick. It's Miss 'Liza and Harry. They've left, and I'm meant to tell you that they're goin' to Canada."

George opened his mouth to respond, then closed it again, finding his voice quite lost. He shook the boy gently instead, urging him with his eyes to get out of there.

But Pete shook his head, still having more to say. "Mas'r Shelby's run into a bad way, 'cording to Eliza. Had some bad debts. Man who owned those debts—one Mas'r Haley—came callin' yesterday, sayin' he wouldn't settle for anythin' other than slaves. Picked out my Pa, Miss 'Liza, plus young Harry. Miss 'Liza said she wouldn't stand for it. Left last night."

Suddenly George realized what it meant. A man had come to buy his son and his wife. Upon hearing about it, Eliza had done the only thing she could do—up and left. But that meant that she was out there on her own with their son, on her way to Canada—chased by who knew how many slave catchers and dogs. Shelby would never send the catchers after her, he thought defensively, but that wasn't the point. If a trader had been after her, and money had exchanged hands, then she didn't belong to Shelby anymore. She belonged to the trader. And he'd never heard of a trader that didn't use slave catchers anytime he felt the need.

"Why didn't Eliza come for me?" he snapped, suddenly angry. "Why didn't you come sooner?"

"She wanted to, but Pa told her there were too many 'trollers 'round here at night," Pete answered quickly. "Said it wasn't safe for her. Pa says you must go after her, Mista George. Haley's been to the big house this mornin', screamin'. Says if Mas'r Shelby don't find Miss 'Liza, he'll go after her himself. He owns the papers to Harry, he says. Says he'll send the dogs."

George nodded firmly. He was already planning on leaving. He'd just have to change his timetable. His family needed him.

"Where are they headed?" he asked.

"Maysville. Miss 'Liza's got her travelin' papers, plans to take a ferry across to Ohio."

"Alone? On foot?" George continued, already devising his route. He didn't have any papers for travel—Harris had taken the ones Wilson had given him—but he could find a way around that. He was sure he could.

Pete nodded, then held out a stack of papers, as if he'd read George's mind. "Pa's travelin' papers, Mista George. He said to give them to you. Says you can pass for him, easy enough, and he won't be…" The boy's voice hitched for a moment, and he looked down at his feet, overcome by emotion. "He won't be needin' 'em where he's goin'."

George took the boy in his arms, remembering suddenly what he'd said. The trader Haley was taking Uncle Tom, though Eliza and Harry had escaped. That meant this boy was losing his father to an unknown fate in an unknown place. They might never see each other again.

"Thank you, Pete. You've been a brave boy today, and I know you'll be brave for your mother, sister, and brother. Now run home to your family. You should be with your father, not me. Give your pa my thanks." He turned and sent the boy running, his heart going after him. To know that one's father was leaving, and to know that you'd never see him again …

His mind flew back to Eliza. He would have to leave right away, and he would have to make good time to catch up with her. Maysville. He knew the town Pete had named—a small place, though it boasted several businesses, thanks to the ferry there. It was the nearest place to cross the Ohio River, and a good choice. The road to Maysville was simple too, but it cut right through the wilds.

Without food or shelter—or even a weapon!—he didn't know if Eliza would make it.

"George, you fool," he muttered softly, going back to his work. If he'd taken them to Canada when he still worked at the factory—as he'd meant to do—none of this would have happened. The trader would never have come for Eliza or Harry, and she would never have run off on her own. They might be safe now, already in Canada, in their own snug little home. Instead, they were separated, with Eliza in the wild by herself but for little Harry.

George bit his lip and swore to himself. He'd leave within the hour, as soon as he was sure William wasn't watching. He'd find his family and get them to Canada, or die trying.

CHAPTER 13

After many, many hours of walking—both on her own and carrying Harry when he grew too tired—Eliza reached the town she recognized as Maysville. She'd been here several times in the past as Mrs. Shelby had friends in the area and often brought Eliza along when she visited.

She'd never walked here on her own, though, trudging over the dusty country roads and through the woods alone. She'd been traveling for almost a full day, she thought, given the position of the sun, and was more tired than she could ever remember being, and cold on top of that, her double layers doing little to protect her from the frigid night.

In short, she'd never been so happy to see a place in her life as she was right then to see Maysville. Now that she'd arrived, she hoped to find some shelter for herself and

Harry—perhaps a place where they could rest for an hour or two until one of the ferries arrived. She remembered from one of her previous visits that a public house sat right on the water, catering to those waiting for the boats, and headed in that direction, praying that her feet would support her until she got there.

The place was small, boasting only two public houses with one short street of businesses, for which she was quite grateful. The buildings sat tightly together, their walls up against one another in a clash of blues and greens. A grocery was first on the corner, its sign advertising fresh eggs, and a seamstress made her living in the building next door. The last building was a farrier, judging by the smell, and must have done well in a town that acted as nothing so much as a gateway to the ferries. At the end of this row sat the first public house—inn and tavern both, if she remembered rightly. That was her destination, and she hurried toward it.

The street was well kept and easier to travel than anything she'd seen in the last day. Within moments she was pushing the front door of the tavern open and looking wearily for the hostess. They were still in slave country, of course, but up here, so close to the border, the people were more generous with people like her. She prayed that the owner of this tavern was, at least.

"Well now, dearie, you look like you've been travelin' awhile," that woman said, bustling suddenly from the kitchen. "And with a young one, no less! How can I help you?"

Eliza tried to pat down and arrange her hair, giving her mind a moment to settle. The woman was going to be friendly then, and praise the Lord for that. "Please, ma'am, my son is awfully sick, and I need to get him to the doctor," Eliza said desperately. "When's the next ferry?"

"Well now miss, the ferries aren't runnin' right now," the woman said kindly. "The ice's still meltin' on the river, ain't room for the boats to get through."

"Oh please, ma'am, surely someone is goin' through?" Eliza asked, her heart breaking. She'd never thought that there might still be ice on the river. But she couldn't stay here, or Haley would find them! "My son is awfully sick. He needs a doctor!"

The woman gave her a long, sympathetic look, then turned back toward the kitchen. "Solomon!" she called out. "Woman here wants to know if anyone's runnin' across the river today!"

A large-bellied man walked out of the kitchen, wiping his hands on his shirt, and looked Eliza up and down. "Well now, heard tell a man might be totin' some barrels over later. He might be able to take you," he said kindly.

Eliza gasped in relief at this news, too happy for words. The hostess mistook her joy for fatigue, though, and moved forward to take her arm.

"Here now, girl, I can see you're quite done in, and your little one's already asleep." She ushered Eliza into a chamber to the side of the main room, gesturing toward the area. "You two take this room for the time being and rest. I'll come find you when that man comes around with his barrels."

Eliza nodded in dazed thanks and stumbled into the room. She was indeed tired, so much so that it nearly made her sick, and Harry had been moaning with cold in his sleep. She moved toward the small bed where she tucked the child under the covers and then took herself to the chair by the window. Here, she could see the street outside and the Ohio River in the background. She'd be able to see if anyone came up the street, though she prayed that they'd be long gone before anyone came after them. If anyone came after them.

Back home they'd be getting ready for lunch, she thought, and she'd be doing Mrs. Shelby's hair. Gossiping about the day. Laughing at something Mr. Shelby had done or said.

She sighed in regret, a wave of homesickness washing over her. They would have found her missing this morning. What had they done about it? What had Haley done when he arrived to find Harry missing?

Little question, really, for she already knew the answer. Haley would have been outraged at the trickery, no doubt blaming Mr. Shelby himself for letting them get away. He would have been raging at her absence. And he would have sent the slave catchers after her, to take her back—or come after her himself, maybe even with dogs. If Mr. Shelby had given him Harry's papers, he would see it as his right, and nothing would stop him.

She hoped only that the man with the barrels got there before Haley did.

CHAPTER 14

George ducked under another branch and let it sweep back to the ground behind him, then looked anxiously around the clearing. He'd been running for what felt like hours now, though it couldn't have been more than one at the most—the sun was still high in the sky, shining down on him.

Should have waited until dark, he thought abruptly, chastising himself for his hurry. Waiting for dark would have meant that he didn't have to deal with broad daylight, and everything that could happen with such visibility. He would have been able to hide in the shadows. Move more quickly. Still, the slave catchers—and their dogs—were out at night, just as they were during the day, and the situation hadn't allowed him the luxury of time. Eliza and Harry were out there somewhere, facing the wilds by themselves.

Running from the slave catchers, seeking safety, and with little more than Eliza's mind to keep them safe.

No, he couldn't have waited until nightfall to go after them. His heart wouldn't have allowed it.

At the thought, he broke into a quick trot again, rushing through the underbrush without care for his newly injured back and hand. As he ran, he thought of only one thing: He must get to them before the slave trader did. He'd never forgive himself if he didn't find them first. The trees and underbrush flew past him, whipping at his face and arms as he darted around and under the low-lying trees. It was a thick forest, at least, and provided many places to hide, should he need them.

Suddenly he pulled to a stop, his chest heaving. Ahead of him stood exactly what he'd been afraid of—two white men, dressed for the outdoors and looking as if they'd been living off the land for some time. They both had pistols pointed right at him. His mind raced, trying to remember what he'd come up with as his official story for being out and on his own, and he cursed himself again for not having waited until dark.

"Get over here, boy!" one of them called harshly. "What're you doin' out here by yourself in the middle of the day?"

George walked slowly toward them. They were headed

south rather than north, which meant they were headed into slave country. Not chasing anyone, then. Perhaps they weren't patrollers or slave catchers after all. Perhaps he could talk his way out of this.

"Morning, Mas'rs, what can good ol' Tom help you with?" he asked in his most subservient voice.

"Where you runnin' off to, boy?" the second man laughed. "What's got you in such an almighty hurry?"

"On urgent business for Mas'r Shelby," George answered quickly. "Surely you know him, large plantation just south of here. I'm ordered up to Maysville to bring his cousin south to the plantation. Got a late start, though, and Mas'r won't tolerate me bein' late. Not to get his cousin."

The two men looked him up and down, taking in his rough dress and worn shoes. The taller one shook his head firmly. "You ain't goin' to get your master's cousin dressed like that, boy. Why, I'd bet my mother's best necklace you've escaped your master, ain't ya? You're runnin' on account of you bein' scared they're going to find you."

The other man laughed a low, wicked laugh and nodded. "Sure do think you're right, Bill. Just look at the fear in that boy's eyes. Why, long as we're out here, and you're out here..." He held his pistol up, his point becoming clear, and George stepped back.

The man named Bill stepped forward. "Right you are, Bob. Figure this boy has a price on his head—least he will when they've discovered he's gone! Turn 'round, boy. We're takin' you home."

George shook his head. "Please, sirs, I ain't lyin'. Look, I've got my travelin' papers right here." He stuck his hand in his pocket and pulled out the papers Pete had given him—Tom's traveling papers—and held them out to the white men, his hand trembling with what he hoped looked like subservience.

Bob took the papers and glanced at them unwillingly. "Travelin' papers, eh? What's your name, boy?"

"Thomas Shelby."

The man snorted. "These here papers don't have that name on them."

George glanced at the papers, terrified that there had been some mix up, and realized—to his relief—that he'd just handed them the papers upside down. The men probably couldn't read very well to start with and obviously didn't know enough to turn the papers around.

"So sorry, Mas'rs, I've handed you the papers all amok," he muttered, reaching out to turn the papers so that they could read the name on them. He pointed to Tom's name, hoping that this would be the end of it. "Right there, sir, Tom Shelby. That's my name."

The men muttered between themselves for a moment, obviously pretending to read the paper, and then looked George up and down one more time. Finally, Bob handed the papers back to George.

"Well then, boy," he said grudgingly, "looks like you got the right to be travelin' through here after all. We won't get nothin' for bringin' back a man with his rightful papers on him. Get you gone, and you make sure you bring your master's cousin back in a timely fashion, you hear?"

"Yes, Mas'r. Thank you, Mas'r," George murmured, ducking his head once in a bow. He turned and headed forward into the forest, doing his best to walk quickly without looking like he was running madly away from the men. He thanked all his lucky stars that Uncle Tom had sent him those papers and that he'd had a story already prepared. But that wouldn't stop the men from chasing after him if they decided to.

He wouldn't be safe until he'd left them far behind.

He frowned as he walked, though, and before long his gratitude became frustration, and then anger, despite the precarious situation. Wasn't this just what he'd been saying to Eliza the last time he saw her? That men like those—those low-bred, illiterate fools!—were allowed to order him, an educated, intelligent man, around as though they owned him? And would have taken him back to Harris, too, if he hadn't had those papers. As if they owned him themselves. As if they had the right to own another man and decide whether he would live or die!

He scowled down at his right palm, which still burned and itched with the "H" branded onto it. A sign, Harris had said, something to remind him who he belonged to. And now he'd never be rid of it, no matter how free he became.

Why? Why were men like that allowed to be free while he had to run for his life, and that of his family? What kind of merciful God would allow such a state of affairs?

"Well, there's different laws up in Canada, aren't there, and those are the only laws I'll be living by now," he told himself, ducking under another branch. But first—first—he had to find Eliza and Harry.

He hoped they were still in Maysville.

CHAPTER 15

Eliza stopped singing and brushed Harry's forehead with her hand. He was sound asleep, poor fellow, though it was the middle of the day. The journey north had exhausted him, and she knew he was far more concerned about their flight than he'd let on. Though he was only three years old, he was a bright child, and he appeared to know that something was amiss.

Still, at least he was asleep for the moment. She didn't know how much time they'd have for rest on their road to Canada and hoped that this sleep would keep him for some time. Standing, she moved toward the window, thinking to get a glimpse of the Ohio River and start her planning. She lifted the curtains, her eyes traveling across the road toward the river, and inhaled sharply.

There, turning onto the main street, was the very man from

whom she was running. He had two of the Shelby field hands with him, Sam and Andy, and they were on horses, looking both dusty and worn from the road. The trader, Haley, was running his eyes back and forth over the road, his mission clear.

He was here to find her, and from the look on his face, he wasn't going to stop searching until he'd done so.

Eliza rushed back to the bed, quickly gathering the things they'd tossed about the room and sticking them back into her small pack and pockets.

"Harry, we have to go," she whispered urgently, shaking him gently to rouse him.

"What? Why, Ma, when we just got here?" the boy murmured sleepily.

"Don't ask questions, boy, just climb up here and be quiet," Eliza whispered, terrified that they were already too late. Haley hadn't seen her, but there was no doubt that they were heading in this direction. Only two inns in this town, and they'd search both of them, this one first.

She lifted her son in her arms and rushed to the door, throwing it open in the face of the surprised hostess.

"I'm sorry, ma'am, and thank you for your hospitality, but we must go," she panted, hurrying past the woman.

"But where're you goin'?" the hostess asked, shocked. "The man goin' across the river isn't here yet!"

Just then, the door flew open and there stood Haley, gazing into the room as though he owned the place. When he saw Eliza, his eyes grew wide, and then angry, and his face turned an alarming shade of red.

"That there's my boy!" he shouted, pointing at Harry. "That woman stole him from me, and I'll have him back!"

"See now, I told you she was a runaway," Solomon said, appearing behind Eliza from the kitchen.

"Never you mind that," the hostess muttered. She turned toward Eliza, blocking Haley's view, and her words came out in a rush. "There's a back door, dear, you run back that way and get as far as you can from this place. I'll slow him as much as I'm able."

Eliza didn't wait to hear any more but turned and dashed back through the kitchen, squeezing past a surprised Solomon, through a gauntlet of ovens and sinks, and then out the back door. It led into an alley, crowded with trash cans and deserted crates, but mercifully lacking in people.

"Ma, what's going on?" Harry whined, squirming in her arms.

Eliza tightened her grip around him and turned toward the

river, praying to her Lord that the alley would lead her to the water and that she would find some way across it. "Hush now, little man, we're going to a better place, but you must hold onto me so that I don't lose you," she whispered. If she could just get across that river, she knew she would be safe. Ohio was a free state, and they wouldn't send her back.

If the man Haley caught her before she got to the river, though, she was done for. Harry would be taken and her life would be forfeit, subject to the laws of the land.

So she ran for her life, dashing past piles of garbage and cartons of old food, ducking down beneath the eaves of the buildings as often as she could, and making for the river. Behind her, she could hear Haley screaming and cursing at her, shouting about how Harry was his property. Interspersed with his screams were the voices of the hostess and Sam, trying to be reasonable with the man. But there would be no reasoning with him, she thought. He wanted her son, and he would be coming after them, come hell or high water.

Then the alley opened up, and she realized that she was indeed on the banks of the Ohio River.

"Ain't got no place to go, girl!" Haley called out behind her, his voice growing closer now. "Ain't no one crossin' that river, not with all that ice! You'd best turn him over now, pray your master'll be forgivin' for what you've done!"

Eliza glanced back at him, the breath whistling in her throat, and then turned back to the river. She would die before she let that man take her son. She would die before she let him take her.

Heaving one deep, shaking breath, she grasped Harry more tightly in her arms, murmured for him to hold tightly, and jumped.

Behind her, Haley screamed. "She's tryin' to kill herself—and my profits!" he shouted. "Get the girl!"

But Eliza was already on the river. By pure luck, she'd landed on a piece of ice large enough to support her. Now she took stock of her situation, balancing precariously on the ice, and found another piece of ice in front of her. There. She could make it, she was certain. She just had to... Without another thought, she crouched and leapt, landing on one foot on the next ice floe.

Her bare feet—for she'd left her shoes in the room at the inn —tore on the sharp ice, and she let out a quick grunt of pain. Glancing down, she could see that she was bleeding heavily and would be wounded when she arrived on the other side of the river. But that didn't matter right now. All that mattered was getting across.

The ice under her began to sink, and she panicked, looking desperately for another piece large enough to support her. Harry was slipping with all the movement, and she hitched him up again, then darted forward and jumped. The ice came up under her and she sobbed in relief, then looked down at her son.

"Get over on my back," she told him quickly. He climbed her obediently, young scamp that he was, and wrapped his arms around her neck. Eliza nodded once. "Hold tight, Harry, for we're playin' a game now," she whispered.

"A game?" he asked, his voice filled with wonder.

"Yes. A game where we jump from ice to ice and must make it to the other side of the river. See the shore there?" She pointed it out but didn't wait for him to answer. "We must get there. You must tell me when you see ice that I can jump to. Are you ready?"

Then, still without waiting for an answer, she flailed herself at another piece of ice, and then another, Harry calling out from time to time, encouraging her. After ten very lucky leaps, they were at the center of the river and over the deepest water. Eliza was exhausted, her feet bleeding freely, and she didn't know how much longer she could carry on. But she could hear Haley screaming behind them, calling out for a boat so that he could come after her, and she knew that she couldn't stop. Not yet.

Not until they were safe.

"Mamma, there!" Harry said suddenly, pointing to the right.

Eliza leapt without thinking, putting her feet out blindly for the ice. She grunted in pain when she landed but kept going, jumping from ice floe to ice floe like the deer she'd seen in the forest, never pausing to think of anything more than her next jump. The other bank was growing closer with each leap, and that became her only thought. She wasn't sure her body was going to hold out much longer, but if she could get there by force of will alone…

When they got to that other bank, her Harry would be safe. It was all that mattered.

Then suddenly, she'd taken her last leap and reached that bank, to stumble up the muddy embankment and collapse, terrified and elated, on the soil there. But her joy didn't last long.

"Girl, what on earth do you think you're doin', runnin' across the river that way?" a deep voice asked.

She looked up, shocked, and found that she was staring into the cold, angry eyes of a white man standing over her.

CHAPTER 16

George was still walking as quickly as he could, taking in the changing scenery around him and hoping he would hit Maysville soon, when he heard the horses ahead of him. He ducked behind a large, hollow tree trunk and crouched down, wondering who he was going to come across this time. To his surprise and relief, the new men were none other than Sam and Andy, two slaves from the Shelby plantation. They didn't have any white men with them, so George stepped out of the trunk and called to them.

"What are you two doin' out here, so far from home?" he called, pleased to see people he knew and trusted. "Where are you comin' from?"

Sam's face lit up with pleasure as well. "There you are! Comin' from Maysville, George, and we were hopin' we'd find you. Just left that man Haley in town. He's on your wife's trail and won't be distracted. Uncle Tom's boy told us you were up this direction, comin' through the woods, and we hoped we'd come across you."

"You came with Haley?" George asked, shocked. "The man huntin' Eliza and Harry? Why'd you let him get here so quick? You know Eliza's on foot!" He held onto his anger, waiting to hear their reasoning. If they were with that man, they could have delayed him until all three of them were safely away.

"Well and we tried, George, you can bet on that," Andy answered. "Put a burr under his horse's saddle, but that only slowed him down a little. Even took him over to the Harris plantation for a time. Told him we were certain that Eliza and Harry were there, hidin' with you."

"At the Harris plantation?" George gasped, half-laughing and half-terrified. If someone had been asking after him there, and that had led Harris to search for him…

"Well, it sounded like a good idea at the time," Sam said quickly, glancing with worry at George's face. "'Course it didn't work out that way, and I can see you're already suspectin' what happened. Harris realized you'd run off soon as Haley started askin' about you, and he was right furious. Gave Haley his carriage for chasin' after you all, put a reward on your head, and gave Haley the names of the two best slave catchers in Kentucky. I'm 'fraid we got you in more trouble, George. Leastwise, Harris discovered you was missin' before he would have."

George opened his mouth to answer, then shut it again. Harris would have discovered his absence eventually, of course, and there was nothing to be done about that. But the man going after Eliza, with slave catchers now…

"Why did you help him get here?" he asked hoarsely.

"We didn't, George," Sam said simply. "Harris told him how to get here."

"And where is he now?"

Andy quickly took George through the happenings of the day, telling him how they'd discovered Eliza and Harry in the public house and how she'd run—with the help of the hostess—toward the river.

"She crossed it by herself, George," he said, his voice awestruck. "Ran right across the ice, as if she was a deer and the ice no more than a grassy meadow. Graspin' your son the whole way, as if her life depended on it. 'Fore we knew it, she was on the other side, safe and clear to go on her own way."

"It was a miracle, and no mistake," Sam added. "We thought

she'd slip and drown, for sure, but she ran right across those chunks of ice. Barely even paused to look around her."

"And are they safe now?" George gasped, afraid to believe this good luck. If they'd got to the other side, they were in free territory, and well ahead of Haley.

Andy shook his head. "We couldn't see too far. Only saw her get to the bank on the other side. Looked like a man met her there. But it was a long way, and we couldn't rightly see."

"And Haley? Did he go after them?"

"No sir," Sam answered, grinning. "Fact is, ain't no ferries or boats runnin' right now, on account of all that ice. And no sane man would try somethin' like what Eliza did. Haley's well and truly stuck in Maysville, fumin' to himself about losin' Harry."

George whooped with joy. This was even better than he'd hoped! Eliza and Harry away and safe, and Haley stuck in Maysville! "Where is he?" he asked.

"Eventually, he'll be at the Borderland Tavern," Sam replied. "Plannin' to arrange a meetin' with the slave catchers there, much good may it do them."

George was moving the second Sam stopped speaking. "I have to get to Eliza and Harry before they do."

Sam put out a hand and grabbed George's arm. "Eliza's in her own trouble," he said. "You need to get back to the Harris plantation 'fore those slave catchers find you. Mas'r Shelby won't have anything done to Eliza, even if they catch her. Harris won't be so kind to you, and you know it."

George pulled his arm from Sam's grasp. "I won't abandon my family, Sam. And I'm not goin' back to that plantation. I'm never goin' back to that life."

"George, you go after them, you'll have twice the slave catchers after you. All three of you'll be caught. You can't help them. And Harris is offerin' more money for you dead than alive. You know what that means."

George paused, taking a moment to deal with that harsh reality. Harris had offered a larger bounty on his death than his live return then. Well, it wasn't the first time it had been done, and it didn't surprise him. In fact, it increased his motivation. If the men of the South valued him more dead than alive, that was all the answer he needed. He was doing the right thing running for Canada, and nothing was going to stop him.

"I don't fear them, Sam, and I won't go back there. Now that's the end of it. I thank you both for your help, and pray that you'll find a safe road back home."

Sam shook his head gently. "If you ain't afraid of them and

what they're goin' to do to you, George, ain't nothin' more we can say. Save your prayers for yourself. You need the safe road more than we do."

With that, Sam and Andy turned and rode away, leaving George quite alone with his thoughts.

"Too afraid to find freedom for themselves," George muttered, staring after them. He would have happily taken them along with him, but they were just like so many others —too full of fear to seek any other life. Too afraid of what might happen if they were caught. Shackled to a future of slavery simply because they couldn't see that there was a way out.

He turned and continued on to Maysville, keeping the name of the tavern in the front of his mind and watching closely for any signs that would indicate he was crossing a state line. The trees were changing—he could see that much—and he was moving into the northern states, where trees with needles replaced the large-leaved trees of the South. He was making good time, he thought, and he'd get there while the sun was still up.

From there, it would be a simple thing to find the tavern he needed and to find the slave catchers themselves. If he could figure out what they were planning, maybe he could stall them and increase his own chances of escape.

CHAPTER 17

George found Maysville, and then the Borderland Tavern, easily enough. This appeared to be the largest tavern in town and sat very close to the landing so that people could rest there while they waited for the ferries. He wondered if Eliza and Harry had run by the tavern as they raced to the river and whether they'd actually stopped here. There had been another, smaller tavern on the main street, and they might have stopped there instead. Had they known that there were slave catchers after them? Had they been scared? Had they wondered if he was coming for them?

Of course, none of those things mattered now because they were safely across the river and on their way. George needed to find his own way across so that he could join them. But as long as he was here, he'd find the slave catchers and do everything he could to stall them.

He snuck into the alley across from the tavern and ducked down behind some crates so that he could see the doorway of the tavern without being seen himself. He watched for some time, growing quickly bored, and began to look around the town itself. It was a clean town, he noted abstractly. A nice place to pass some time with your family, perhaps, while you waited to travel to Ohio. If he were white, he'd bring his own family here to take advantage of the taverns.

His eyes traveled back to the tavern then, and he noticed a man that matched Sam's description of Haley walking out into the evening's light. He stretched and gazed across the street as if he had nowhere else to be, then turned with a frown and walked back into the tavern.

"Meeting with the slave catchers, no doubt," George murmured. He'd wait here, he thought, to follow Haley when the man left.

Then he thought better of it. If he could see what the other men looked like, he realized, he'd have a better chance at stopping all of them. He stood and crossed the street, hoping he looked as if he belonged there, and walked right up to the door of the tavern. He'd never be allowed inside, he assumed, on account of the color of his skin and well-worn slave clothes, but no one was going to stop him from standing there and gazing in. He could say he was looking for his master or something like that.

He slid around the doorjamb and gazed inside, his eyes slowly adjusting to the darker room. Before he could see much, though, a well-dressed man who looked to be the manager of the place barged through the door. The man noticed George and pointed a stern finger at him, as if he knew who George was and what he was doing.

George tensed, ready to run at the first hint of trouble. The last thing he needed was to be caught now and turned over to some slave catchers.

"Where've you been, Francis?" the man asked, much to George's surprise. "If Jacobs is goin' to continue rentin' his slaves out as servers, he better make sure you get here on time. Why're you late, boy?"

George tried to answer, but found his voice lost to his surprise.

The man in front of him shook his head abruptly, discounting anything George was going to say. "Well it's plain you're 'bout to lie to me 'bout where you've been, so don't bother," he muttered. "But I'll tell you, I expect you to work as hard for me as you do for Jacobs. I find you lazin' about on the job, I'll punish you same as your master does. You upset any of the customers or drop any food or drink, you'll wish you were back home. I catch you stealin', drinkin', or eatin' while you're here, and that's the end of it. Understand?"

George nodded mutely, realizing that he didn't actually have to answer the man, who had obviously mistaken him for someone else. Still, working here as a server would give him the opportunity to spy on Haley more easily. Perhaps this was a fortuitous mistake after all.

"You understand me, boy? That darkie brain of yours takin' this in?"

George nodded. "Yes sir. Won't disappoint you, sir," he said meekly.

The man lifted an eyebrow in question—or possibly agreement—and turned, walking back into the darkness of the tavern. George grinned to himself at his good luck, then stooped his shoulders a bit and followed the manager.

CHAPTER 18

Eliza drew back, shaking, and sank into the cold mud, staring at the man above her. She didn't recognize him, and she wouldn't, being from the other side of the river. But why was he looking at her with such anger?

"Please, sir, I'm just tryin' to get my son to the doctor," she whispered, hoping he would take pity on them.

He reached down a reluctant hand and helped her to her feet. "What on God's green earth are you doing, woman?" he asked, now looking more surprised than angry. "You could have been killed, acting so recklessly!"

Eliza felt herself blush and cast her eyes back across the river. The pieces of ice weren't nearly as close as she had thought they were, she could see that now, and dark was falling quickly, hiding the other side of the river—and the man who'd been chasing her. "Didn't have a choice, sir. Had to get my son to this side of the river. This is my boy, my Harry." She held the child forward, praying he would smile for the man. "And I'm Eliza."

The man shook his head. "Don't tell me any more, girl, if you know what's good for you. I don't want to know your name. Knowing your name would mean I'd have to answer anyone asking after you. And I won't tell you mine either. I don't want you knowing my name any more than I want to know yours."

"Well, I'm sorry to hear it, sir, but I understand your reasoning. I'll just be goin' then." She turned to head up the bank, thinking she'd head for the small wooded area she saw at the top of the slope, but she stopped when she felt his hand on her arm.

"Where you going, girl? There are many doctors in Kentucky. You don't look badly treated. Why're you running?"

Eliza's heart broke a little at the question, and she glanced down at her bare, torn feet. "I wasn't badly treated, sir. Love my master and mistress somethin' fierce. But they were forced to sell my boy, and I couldn't see him go." She glanced up, knowing that her tears showed in her eyes, even in the growing dark. "Do you have a son, sir?"

The man nodded.

"And what would you do, sir, if someone was tryin' to take him from you, send him to a place where you'd never see him again? A place where you didn't know if he'd be safe, or fed, or even killed?"

"I would die fighting for him," the man answered softly, understanding dawning across his face. "I'd never let anyone take him from me."

"And that's just what I'm doin'," she answered, her voice firm. "I'm runnin', and I'll die if I must, but I won't let them take him."

"Well, and I understand that," he finally answered. "But I can't help. The new Fugitive Slave Act would give me six months in prison and a thousand dollars in fines if I helped you." He paused for a long moment, looking deeply into her eyes, and her heart began to hammer in her chest. He wasn't going to help, that was clear, but would he let her go?

Or would he take her and turn her in for what she'd done?

"I see you're dead scared, and you've every right to be, but I won't turn you in," he said, seeming to read the questions in her mind. "Anyone with enough grit to jump across a river of ice deserves their freedom. And if you'd do that to save your son...well, I can't say I blame you."

Eliza fell against him and sucked in gulps of the ice-cold air, the tears coming hot and quick to her eyes. "Oh sir," she murmured, "you don't know how relieved I am to hear that! Thank you sir, thank you."

The man gave her a kind look. "Now child, there's no need to thank me. Any Christian man would do the same. But where will you go? What will you do?"

"I'm goin' to Canada," Eliza answered, her shoulders coming up in a sudden feeling of strength and determination. She glanced around, taking in for the first time the difference in the land here. Gone were the wide, gently rolling hills of the South. Beyond the trees, she could see sharp, craggy mountains covered in dark green trees. Their tips were capped in snow and a mist was rolling down their slopes toward the river. She shivered at the thought, suddenly feeling how meager the two dresses she wore would be against that cold.

Still, what choice did she have? She must go on, she must! "My husband's headed to the North, and I'm goin' to find him, so that we can make a life together. Keep our son safe."

"Well, there are abolitionists in Ripley," he said slowly. "They might help you. Give you your path at least."

Eliza took a deep breath. "Then I'm headin' for Ripley," she said. "Can you tell me the way?"

"I can, but you must take care," the man answered, "for there are some abolitionists there, but most people in Ripley are not. And many would turn you in quicker than they'd help you. Come, I shall point you in the right direction."

So saying, he took her hand and led her and Harry away from the riverbank, up the slope and toward the trees. Eliza followed, her feet slipping and sinking into the freezing mud below her, her mind racing with both discovery and fear. To Ripley, then. But would George find her there? Would she find Canada at all? Or would she find herself—and Harry—in chains and heading back to an unknown fate on the plantations of the South?

CHAPTER 19

George glanced around the room, taking in the general sense of well-fed satisfaction. There was a roaring fire in the large fireplace to his left, and the open space of the room held several tables of various size and shape, each playing host to a number of raw-boned outdoorsmen. Although these men fit a number of physical descriptions, they were dressed—nearly to a man—in animal furs and leather, their boots worn from striding through the forests of the country. In the corner, a number of young Negro boys rolled around together, likely awaiting their masters' commands, and with them lay one or two large dogs. Not the type that would be hunting an escaped slave, he noted quietly, rather the kind more often used for raccoons and foxes.

George breathed a quick sigh of relief at this and moved into the warm, smoky room after the manager, who had told George to call him Mas'r Isaacs. His eyes roamed across the room, searching for the man Sam and Andy had described to him, for that was his quarry. That was the man he needed to find. And stop.

Before he found him, though, Isaacs dragged him into a back room and handed him a stack of clothes. "Here, boy, you'll wear these when you're workin' here. And don't you get 'em dirty, or I'll take the price of launderin' 'em out o' your wages, see if I don't."

George grimaced and looked down. The man had handed him a clean white shirt and a pair of black trousers. He could see quite clearly that the clothes had been worn before—and often—but they were cleaner and nicer than the clothing he currently wore.

"And gloves, Mas'r?" he asked quickly, thinking of his branded hand, which still hadn't begun to heal and hurt if he used it too often. If someone saw it, however, the punishment would be severe. "Surely you've got gloves to match this shirt, keep the plates clean."

The man frowned, but nodded once at this logic, and turned to rummage through a drawer for gloves. After a moment, he turned around with a pair of white gloves in his hand. "First Negro I ever saw that asked for gloves," he noted. "Have to say I approve of the sentiment, boy." He handed

George the gloves, then gestured back out the door. "You'll go and take orders, serve food and drink, clean up after the patrons, and keep the customers happy. You got that?"

"Yes, sir," George answered, ducking his head. He stepped into the back corner, slipped out of his slave pants, and donned the new trousers. He put the new white shirt on over his slave shirt because he didn't want any blood from his back to stain it. To his surprise, they fit like they had been made for him, and had almost no damage. He slipped the gloves on as well, scowling in pain as the fabric scraped against his brand, and a moment later he was back out in the main room, ready to begin.

It took only a matter of seconds for him to find Haley. He was sitting at a shadowed table in the corner of the room with two men, smoking cigars. George watched them for a moment, noted that they had mugs of ale in front of them but no food, and walked quickly toward them. One of the men was small, he noted, his face clever and rat-like, while the other man was very large and could be described only as a brute. Neither was an outdoorsman—not traditional hunters, these two—but the larger man was very obviously accustomed to some sort of physical labor. This second man was the one that would come after him, George thought. He had the look of someone who used his fists first and asked questions later.

Fortunately, the man didn't look like he used his mind at all. The low brow and slightly drooping lips gave him a stubborn, but unintelligent, demeanor. Determined, but not smart, George thought wryly. It would be a simple thing to outthink such a man.

He walked to the table behind the men and began to gather mugs and clean the table itself as he listened to Haley's conversation with these men.

"You boys enjoyin' those cigars?" Haley asked sharply. "Enjoyin' that gin?"

"Well enough," the large man answered slowly.

"Well then, now that I've treated you with them, shall we get down to business?" Haley asked, his eagerness obvious even to George's ears. "Loker, lookin' at you, I can see you takin' to slave catchin'. But Marks, I must say I can't imagine you doin' well in the business."

George stifled a snort. Loker and Marks were their names, then, and though he hated to do it, he had to agree with Haley—the large man looked well accustomed to slave catching, while the small man looked as though he belonged in an office, not the outdoors.

"Well, sir, the fact is we both have talents essential to the catching of slaves," the small man responded in a sharp, nasal voice. "Loker here is in charge of thumping, fighting, beating, catching, and frightening, so to speak. I, on the other hand, specialize in speculating, thinking, planning, strategizing, and handling the money. Surely you can see the difference."

"Marks' job's the lyin'," Loker added with a harsh laugh.

"Well, call it what you want, but there isn't any person in this country that can swear to something better than I can," Marks responded arrogantly. "I can put on a long face and weave a story that'll make any justice of the court weep, and well you know it."

George took a sharp breath. So that was their game. Catch the runaways, then take them to court and swear that they belonged to this small gentleman. It wasn't the first time he'd heard of that but—

"Boy, what's takin' you so long with that table?" Isaacs asked suddenly, having approached George from the other side.

George looked up, caught off guard, and realized he'd been standing quite still—and listening rather than working. "Just bein' thorough, Mas'r, since this is the first I've done," he answered.

"Well, that table's clean enough. You get over there, ask those gentlemen if they need anythin' else," Isaacs snapped.

He gestured toward Haley and his party, making it clear where he expected George to go, and George nodded humbly.

"Yes, sir." He slid toward the other table and nodded gently toward the men there. "Get you sirs anythin' else?" he asked, glancing at them from beneath his lashes. They'd be easy enough to identify, he thought, should he see them on the street. Or in the wilds.

"Long's Haley's payin', I'll take two more drinks. And another cigar," Loker said. He handed George his tumbler, which was empty.

"And I'll take another mint julep," Marks added in his rat-like tone.

Haley harrumphed at this additional expense but gestured for George to do as they said. George turned and headed toward the kitchen, his mind turning over this strange turn of events. Serving the very people who were after his wife and child—it was the perfect opportunity to mislead them, send them in the wrong direction. But how to do it?

By the time he returned with the drinks, he thought he had a general idea.

"And that, gentlemen, is what happened," Haley was just

saying. George's ears pricked up, and he wondered if the man was talking about Eliza and Harry.

"She just jumped across the river like a skipping stone?" Marks asked, surprise obvious on his face. George almost had to swallow his tongue to keep from saying anything as he came to a standstill on the other side of the table.

Haley nodded. "T'was the damndest thing I ever saw," he answered.

Loker grabbed his drinks from George, who stood frozen at the connection to Eliza, and downed the first in one gulp. "Well, we're on the job now. We'll get those three slaves back to their masters, one way or another."

Haley sat back as though satisfied. "Well, I'd be much obliged, friend."

George brought himself back to life then and leaned over the table to pour water into the water glasses. As he did, he noticed Marks' eyes on him, full of wonder. And suspicion.

"Haley, you said that Harris boy George was tall and hand-some, didn't you? And light skinned? Like this boy here?"

"Yes, and with an H branded on his right palm."

Marks narrowed his eyes, his glance moving down to George's gloves, and George drew back quickly.

"Got anythin' of the girl's for the bloodhounds?" Loker asked suddenly.

Haley laughed. "Sure do. Girl left her scarf at the public house today, 'long with her shoes. Got the scarf right here in my bag."

George jerked at this, shocked, and the pitcher of water—which he still held aloft over the table—jerked with him, sloshing water over the table and onto Marks' lap. Marks yelped in surprise and began to fuss with the tablecloth, trying to use it to dry himself off.

Suddenly Isaacs was back at the table, furious. "So sorry, sir," he said to Marks, handing him a dry cloth. He turned on George and pushed him once, his face flaming with anger.

"I have to come out here after you again, boy, and I'll have you strapped to that whippin' tree, you understand me? And when I'm done, I'll send you home to Jacobs with your own explanation 'bout why you didn't get paid."

Nodding, George took the proffered cloth and began to clean up the water, ducking down to the floor and out of sight of the men at the table. His back ached at the movement, and he wondered suddenly if his back wounds were bleeding again.

"Well, we'll have to keep the dogs on their leashes," Marks said as he dried himself. "Otherwise they'll rip the girl and her lad apart when they catch her."

"You worry too much 'bout the welfare of the darkies," Loker said.

"Be that as it may, I've got an idea that keeping the girl pretty and unscarred is important," Marks shot back.

"And what's that?" Haley asked gleefully.

"Tell us again how pretty she is, Haley."

"First-class beauty, and no mistake," Haley said quickly. "Shapely girl, caramel complexion, and smooth skin. Been raised right, too, with pretty manners and a clear voice."

Marks hummed in response, and George froze under the table. What were they planning now? That was his wife, for goodness sake! His temper began to burn, slow and hot, but he tamped it down. This certainly wasn't the time for reckless actions.

"Well now Haley, seeing as how you're only after the boy, and since we're going to catch all three of them, seems fair that we should send the father back to Harris, give the boy to you, and get the girl for ourselves. Sell her down the river to New Orleans, eh Loker, where they have special work for beautiful Negresses."

George clenched his teeth until they hurt, just to keep from attacking the men. He would have strangled the little man if he could. Sell Eliza down the river! Just like Harris did to his sister, Charlotte. The very thought broke his heart and drove a stake deep into his mind. Why, he'd die before he allowed that to happen.

"Fine idea, Marks, that's why I keep you around," Loker said, laughing.

"But what about Shelby?" Haley asked. "He'll expect me to return his girl, and no mistake."

"If Shelby finds out, he can go lookin' for her. If he finds us, we just—" George heard a fist bang onto the table and a shout of laughter, "— finish the matter." It was Loker, and his point was clear—he didn't plan to return Eliza to Shelby, and he didn't intend to explain himself to Shelby at all.

There was a long pause, and then Haley spoke again. "Yes, yes, I see your point. And my cut of the girl's sale?"

"Zero."

"Now see here, that's not fair at all! I've put you on to the girl, haven't I?"

"Well now Haley, Marks and I're doin' the catchin', aren't we? And we could catch all three of them and sell the lot.

Cut you out completely. Seems to me we're doin' you a favor, givin' you the boy."

Haley sputtered, and George bit his tongue again. The thought of these men getting their hands on his wife and child sent a cold chill up his spine and set his wounds aching. The idea that they would try to sell both Eliza and Harry down the river was almost more than he could bear.

"Well, you don't leave me much choice," Haley finally said.

"Good," Loker answered. "Then you won't give us any trouble."

George brushed hurriedly at the water on the ground, remembering suddenly that he was supposed to be working, and glanced around for any other mess. He needed to get out of this tavern and find Eliza and Harry. This was worse than he'd imagined it could be. The sooner he found them, the sooner they could run for Canada and find their freedom.

"Boy!" Isaac's voice suddenly rang out. George stopped what he was doing, seeing that the manager's feet had joined those of the men around the table. George stood slowly, wondering what the man wanted now. Next to him, the manager had another Negro. George frowned.

"Yes, sir?" he asked.

Isaacs gestured to the man next to him. "This man here says his name is Francis Jacobs. Same as you. Only he's got travelin' papers say the same thing. Where's your travelin' papers, boy?"

"I knew it!" Marks shouted. "I knew there was something off about that boy! Those gloves—"

George didn't wait to hear the rest of the sentence. He dropped the mop and ran for the door.

CHAPTER 20

Eliza arrived in Ripley, Ohio, in the evening, though the winter sun had already sunk behind the mountains around the town. She'd followed the kind man's directions exactly, but it had still taken her longer than he had said to make her way from the river to this town, and now both she and Harry were shivering with cold in the winter night. Harry's coat was keeping him as warm as possible, while the exertion of walking—and carrying her son—kept Eliza's blood circulating, but they needed to find a place to stay, and soon. The night air hadn't damaged them too much in the South, but here, in what she thought of bluntly as the North, the chill of the dark might well kill them. She walked onto the main street and gazed around, her vision clouded with exhaustion. What she saw frightened her, but also gave her hope.

It was a large, bustling city, much larger than those she was used to, and certainly more modern than Maysville. The street played host to at least ten different carriages, carts, and wagons, all hitched to one or two horses, and the sidewalks, though not crowded, did hold a number of people. Even at this late hour, it seemed, the people of Ripley were up and about their business. Turning to the buildings, she saw that there was a newspaper office—which seemed to double as a printer—a general grocer, a farrier, and some sort of hat shop, all there for the offering. On the other side of the street were a hotel and a larger inn with a tavern attached to it. Surely a modern town like this would hold more modern, forward-thinking people.

She ducked down an alley and came quickly to the next street. This one was smaller and—she thanked her stars—held homes rather than businesses. This was where she would start, then—a street where she could meet with families rather than business owners—for Eliza had a plan: Find a family that would help her and beg them to tell her the way to Canada. Beg them to give her food and shelter, if they would, and perhaps a warmer coat for her son.

"But how to tell which is an abolitionist home and which isn't?" she asked herself quietly, glancing from one house to the next. The man had said that there were both abolitionists and non-abolitionists in this city, but how was she to tell the difference? What if she asked the wrong person and they turned her in to the local slave catchers, rather than helping her?

She unconsciously gripped Harry tighter at the thought, and he began to squirm.

"Mamma, when are going back home?" he asked plaintively. "When are we going home? I want to see Mas'r Shelby and Missis, I do."

Eliza heaved a deep sigh, trying to decide whether she could tell him any more than she already had. "Boy, I've already told you that we can't go back there," she murmured. "There's a man that wants to take you away from me, and God alone knows where he'd take you. Mas'r and Missis... well, this bad man has captured them, and he won't let them go unless he finds you. So you see, we can't go back there because if we do, he'll find you. I can't let that happen, so we have to go someplace where that man would never think to look."

"But Mamma—"

"Hush now, boy, God will deliver us and we must have faith. We'll go back and see them one day, I promise. Don't argue with your mother, now, for we must find some people to help us. Help me look for houses where nice people live."

She gave herself a mental shake as well, hoping to shore up

her own determination, for she was tired, thirsty, hungry, and more than a little scared. They'd been on the road for almost twenty-four hours. They hadn't drunk much water and had long since run out of food. Worse, she hadn't slept a wink since leaving the plantation, and she felt her reserves starting to grow thin. But she couldn't stop. Not now. She was Harry's only hope for reaching Canada, and if she gave up…

No. She wouldn't even allow herself to think it. She had to go on. Straightening her shoulders at the thought, she walked briskly toward the door of the first home on the street and knocked. A man opened the door—fairly well-to-do, given his clothing. He looked Eliza up and down once and closed the door again before she could even speak.

Surprised, Eliza stared at the closed door for a moment before turning on her heel and heading for the next house. "Well then, better that he doesn't say anything than to listen to my story, waste my time, and then turn me away," she muttered.

She climbed the steps to the next house and lifted her hand to knock softly. Next to her, the curtains in the window twitched, and Eliza was surprised to see a woman there, holding a candle aloft to see who was at her front door. The woman took one glance at Eliza and scowled, then gestured hurriedly for Eliza to move on.

Eliza's heart sank at this new sign of rejection, but she nodded and moved on. As she went from house to house, though, and neared the end of the street, she began to lose hope. No one had shown her any kindness yet, and most hadn't even spoken to her. Many of the people looked frightened to see her on their doorstep and glanced around as if they suspected a trap. She'd grown up in the warm, easy generosity of the Shelbys and couldn't understand this behavior. What had the people so frightened?

"Must be that new law," she told herself. "People's too scared to help a woman like me, for fear of what might happen to them if they do." She sighed, her heart beginning to break, and wondered what she would do if she didn't find any of the abolitionists. She didn't know the way to Canada from here, or how to get over the border if she did get there. They were out of food, her shoes were long since lost, and she could feel Harry shivering in her arms.

A keen desperation set in, and for a moment she almost thought she should turn and go home. At least she knew she had a home there and had never gone hungry. But she decided that she would try one more house and then sit down to rest and reorder her thoughts. To her surprise, this door was answered by a Negro woman, whom Eliza assumed to be a servant. The woman was large and very dark, but she had a kind face, with wide-set, very intelligent eyes.

"Please, miss, we need help," Eliza said, hoping at least to find a sympathetic soul. "We've been walkin' for days and have no food or water left. But we must get to Canada. We must."

"Well dearie, I can't help you with that," the woman answered, not unkindly. "I just work here, see. Can't let you in or get you anythin' to eat, or I'll be out of a job. But just you walk two blocks that way—" she gestured to the left, the way Eliza had been going, "— and see the people at the church. Maybe someone there'll help."

Eliza put out a hand. "Please, ma'am, I'm just lookin' for some food and water for my boy here. A place to sit for a moment. I'm so tired."

But the woman shook her head and started to close the door, seemingly having given Eliza all she could. Eliza took another desperate step forward, feeling faint at the idea of the warmth and food inside.

Then, quite suddenly, everything went black.

CHAPTER 21

George darted through the kitchen of the tavern, knocking aside both people and furniture as he went, his heart hammering at his ribs. Those men were after him—he could tell by the cursing and pounding of footsteps in the main room—but he couldn't let them catch him. They had no proof of who he was now, but it would take only one glance at the "H" branded on his right palm and it would all be over. He'd be sent back to the Harris plantation where he'd be punished and probably killed.

And Eliza and Harry would still be out there in the wilds, on their own.

He rushed through the back door, cursing that brand and all it stood for, and darted into the darkness of the alley. Thank God it was night out—at least the darkness would give him better cover. He stretched out up to his full height and pushed his legs faster and faster, darting past piles of trash and stacks of goods, between carts and under horses' heads in his panic to get away.

Behind him, he could hear Haley and Loker shouting, though it sounded like Marks had stayed behind. Or perhaps he was up ahead, setting a trap. At the thought, George took a sudden turn down the next alley, heading left —toward the woods, if he remembered correctly. There he'd find trees and, he hoped, a better place to hide. The woods had been thick around the town, with plenty of growth along the ground. He would climb a tree if he had to, to hide there in the darkness and foliage until Haley and his friends had moved on.

By the time he got to the trees, his lungs were burning and his legs had started cramping. Though he'd been working the fields for some time now, his body still hadn't grown used to strenuous physical activity, and this sudden sprint, with no food in his belly, was growing difficult. He darted through the trees and bushes, turning haphazardly left and then right, and finally came to a standstill against the back of an old, rotten trunk. *Should I climb a tree?* he wondered. Perhaps getting up off the ground would give him a better chance.

He shook his head a moment later. That would be sheer stupidity. If the slave catchers found the tree he'd climbed, he'd be well and truly trapped, with no way out of it. And he couldn't jump from tree to tree, like a squirrel. Even if he did, they would see him doing it. No, better to stay on the ground where he could at least run if he saw them coming.

Settling on this plan of action, he ducked down into the shadows at the base of the tree and duck-walked toward the nearest set of bushes. He'd hide there, in the shadows and the brush, and pray that Haley and his friends passed him by. They didn't have any dogs with them, he didn't think, and wouldn't be able to see him in the dark. If he could last here until morning…

Suddenly Haley, Loker, and Marks—who seemed to have joined his friends—called out from quite near him. "George Harris, we've caught ya and you've got no place to run!" one of the men shouted. "Things'll go easier for ya if ya come out now!"

George bit his lip harder than he realized and had to stifle a gasp of pain. They were closer than he'd thought. Thank God he'd hidden when he did.

"Come out, boy, for we'll find you either way!" one of the other men—Loker, George thought—bellowed. "If we have to search, you'll regret it, mark my words!"

George scoffed silently at that. He was in a bad position, true enough, but did they actually think he was going to emerge and give himself up, just like that? Things were going to go badly for him if they got him, regardless of whether he'd turned himself in—he had no doubt about that. Harris had offered more money for his death than his live return, and that was all that would matter to them. If they did get him, he'd have to pray that they killed him quickly, rather than taking their time.

And he'd never been a man to give up easily—particularly not where his own life was concerned.

He ducked down farther, seeking deeper shadow, and decided that he'd wait them out. They were passing him now, at least ten feet to his left, and heading in the direction he'd been taking before he hid.

Lucky I ducked down when I did, he thought wryly. If he'd still been running, he'd be making enough noise for them to pinpoint exactly where he was. And it looked like they'd already nailed down his general direction—they must think he was heading for something specific and that they'd cut him off before he got there. As it was, however, he was silent and hidden, and they were at a loss. Without dogs, they had no way of tracking him. They searched for what felt like at least an hour, then, mumbling to themselves, headed back toward town.

"But he's out here someplace," Haley was saying desperately.

Loker began laughing. "And why does that concern you so much? You don't need to find that boy. You want the girl, or rather, her child, don't you? He's the one belongs to you, ain't he?"

"Well yes, of course, but—"

"And once we have them, mark me, that boy'll come lookin' for 'em. He's the type of Negro that can't stand to have his wife and child in chains when he's free. They've got funny ideas about that. Think they can save their people. We get that girl and the child, that boy'll come 'round to find 'em."

There was a long, pregnant pause and then Haley laughed. "Well, and I suppose you're right, Loker. That's why you're the expert, eh?"

Loker laughed in agreement, then broke the laugh off. "'Sides," he said gruffly, "sooner we find that girl, sooner I can enjoy her myself 'fore we sell her down the river. Tell the buyers what to expect, eh?"

George felt his temper rising at the last statement and gripped his hands together so hard that he thought he might break his own fingers. How dare the man speak that way of Eliza, that sweetest of all sweet women? He clenched his teeth, though, reminding himself that he couldn't fight, not now. He was lucky to have avoided capture.

For now, he needed to think hard and figure out a way across the Ohio River so that he could find Eliza and protect her from men like that. Find his own freedom, and a free life for his wife and child. He would get to the river, he decided, find a ferry, and stow away. It was the quickest, easiest way to get to his family.

CHAPTER 22

Eliza woke up screaming Harry's name. She didn't know what exactly the dream had been, but she was sure that she'd seen him in trouble. In the forest, she thought, being chased by faceless men with guns. And dogs —she could still hear them howling in her memory.

She sat up, chest heaving, and glanced around. A kitchen she didn't recognize, though it was warm and brightly lit, a fire burning merrily in the fireplace and a kettle bubbling on the stove. Her stomach growled loudly at the thought of tea—or any food, for that matter—and the dream began to fade. A house. She was in a kitchen somewhere—but where?

And where was Harry?

At that moment, a bright-eyed, middle-aged Negro woman walked brusquely through the door and pulled up at the sight of Eliza sitting and blinking in the light. She blinked once, then shook her head and smiled.

"Well now, dearie, I'm glad to see you're awake," she said kindly. "Took quite a fall, you did, and what else was I to do but bring you in here to the fire?"

Eliza paused, trying to place the woman, and remembered quite suddenly that she'd seen her earlier, as she was knocking on doors. This had been the woman who opened the door for her and recommended the church. "You brought me in?" she asked numbly. "But where—"

"Oh, your boy's over yonder," the woman replied, gesturing toward the fire. "Old Cudjoe's helpin' him get warm."

Eliza turned to look back toward the fireplace, confused, and realized that Harry was indeed there, sitting in an old Negro man's lap, his face turned to the fire. He looked warmed and thoroughly contented, despite the fact that he was sitting with an absolute stranger. When Eliza exclaimed in surprised relief, he turned toward her, his face lighting up with joy. He jumped from the old man's lap and ran toward her, his arms outspread, to leap into her lap instead.

"Mamma, I've had bread and milk, and there's such a nice fire here. Can't we stay?" the boy asked plaintively.

Eliza laughed at this precocious statement and covered his

face in kisses, squeezing him tightly to her. The fire was indeed warm, and she could feel her senses beginning to sharpen. "Boy, I thought I lost you," she murmured. "I had the most terrible dream, and I was certain I'd wake to find you gone."

A snort from the corner of the room drew her attention, and she was surprised to see an older white man and woman—presumably his wife—seated in the sitting area of the kitchen. She flushed.

"Mas'r, Missis, do excuse my sudden appearance," she mumbled, standing up and bobbing a quick curtsy.

"Now girl, there aren't any masters here in Ohio," the Negro woman said kindly. "This is Senator and Mrs. Bird. You fainted in their house. Or at least on their doorstep. And I'm Aunt Dinah." The woman walked over and pressed Eliza back into her seat, patting her firmly on the back.

"M— my name is Eliza, and this is my son, Harry," Eliza responded, surprised at this turn of events. They'd made it into a home, then, and with people who hadn't protested at their maid—cook?—bringing her into the house. People who were now sitting there, looking kindly at her, as if she was a child to be taken care of. Would they allow her to stay, for the moment? Or better, help her and Harry get to Canada?

"Well dear, you're amongst friends now, so don't worry your pretty little head," Mrs. Bird responded. She stood and walked toward the kettle, which was whistling. "We'll care for you as much as we can, won't we, Mr. Bird?"

Eliza glanced from the kind woman to her husband, who wore rather the opposite expression. In fact, she was horrified to see he looked rather angry, with a stern scowl on his well-lined face.

Mrs. Bird coughed, calling Eliza's attention back, and gestured toward Dinah. "Dinah, why don't you get Eliza and Harry some supper. And make certain it's hot. Nothing warms a body like warm food." She gave Eliza a long, considering stare, which ran from her head to her feet. "And doctor that poor girl's legs and feet," she added. "She's not going to go anywhere with those wounds. We'll have to see what we can do to make her continued journey easier."

Dinah nodded and brought Eliza a plate of fried fish, with mashed potatoes on the side. "Just you eat that, dearie, while I have a look at those feet." The woman knelt down and began to bathe Eliza's feet, while Eliza—wondering at this strange stroke of luck—began to eat. The food tasted divine, no doubt due to her hunger, and she handed pieces to Harry, encouraging him to eat as well.

As she spooned the first bite of potatoes into her mouth, she was surprised to hear the master and mistress—Senator and Mrs. Bird, she reminded herself—arguing in the corner. They were being as quiet as they could, but it was obvious that they disagreed over something. She leaned toward them, hoping that she wasn't the cause of the argument.

Of course, once she could make out their words, she found that she was, in fact, the subject of the disagreement.

"Mary, we must turn her in to the authorities, and you know it as well as I do," Senator Bird said sharply.

"John, we'll do no such thing," Mrs. Bird returned, her voice just as sharp as his.

"But I'm a senator, and a senator who voted for the Fugitive Slave Act at that."

The woman nodded firmly. "Exactly. No need to compound that mistake by making another."

Eliza's heart leapt into her throat, and she nearly choked on the potatoes in her mouth. Why, they were talking about sending her back! And this man had actually voted for the very law that would make her life forfeit. She swallowed with difficulty, wondering how difficult it would be to get out of this house. Perhaps her path hadn't been as lucky as she'd thought.

"Now Mary, that wasn't a mistake, and it's not right for you to say it was. Our brothers in the South want to keep their slaves in the South. As they should—we want no part of that institution up here. This law will keep them satisfied, keep the country out of trouble."

"And when did man get to put his interests before God's?" Mrs. Bird snapped. "God commands that we treat every man as our friend, and yet those men in the South are telling us that we must not. Telling us that we must treat those men and women as possessions, no better than animals, simply because of the color of their skin! It's not right, and well you know it. Turning away an abused woman because she's colored is un-Christian. I won't do it, John."

"Abused! Did you see her hands? She looks as though she's never worked a day in her life!"

"Happy slaves don't run away, John," the woman returned. "She was living a life of servitude, and I don't blame her for leaving. I would have done the same thing myself, if someone took to telling me what to do. God alone knows what might have happened to her!"

"Well, why speculate if you can ask her yourself?" he said roughly, seeming to give in for the time being.

With that, the two of them stood and walked slowly toward Eliza. She watched them come, uncertain whether she should be hopeful or terrified.

Mrs. Bird dropped to her knees at Eliza's side, looking hopefully up at her. "We'd like to help you, but can you tell us where you've come from?"

"Kentucky," Eliza answered hesitantly.

"But how? The boats aren't crossing the river, with all that ice," the senator answered.

"I jumped across the ice on my own, sir."

At this, everyone stopped what they were doing and turned to her, shocked. "Jumped across the ice?" everyone in the room said, nearly in unison.

Eliza nodded. "Yes. I knew I had to do it, and God helped me across. It was that or lose my boy."

"Are you a slave?" the senator asked quietly, as if he was afraid of the answer.

"Yes sir, I was."

"Was your master unkind? Did he abuse you?"

"No sir, Mas'r and Missis were very kind. I've been with them my whole life. They're like parents to me," she answered sadly, for her heart still ached for the Shelbys.

The man turned triumphantly toward his wife. "See there, Mary, I was right!"

Mrs. Bird, however, ignored him. "If they were kind, why did you go through such danger to leave them?" she asked.

Eliza paused. She'd heard their argument and knew that the senator wanted to turn her in to the authorities, while Mrs. Bird was more inclined to help. She knew that Senator Bird had voted for the Fugitive Slave Act, which fined anyone who helped an escaped slave. The senator would have to be careful, just because of his profession. With that in mind, she thought she'd best appeal to the woman before the man could have his way. It was time then. She needed to share something that she'd only shared with a few people.

"Ma'am," she said quietly, "have you ever lost a child?"

At the question, Senator Bird turned and walked slowly to the other side of the room, and tears sprang into Mrs. Bird's eyes.

"Yes, I've lost a little one," she answered, her voice shaking. "Just a month ago, we lost our little boy. He was the same age as your Harry there. Why?"

Eliza sighed. "Before I had Harry, I lost two children. One after another. Both were miscarriages. The first was early in the pregnancy, but the second was late. Late enough that I'd felt her kicking. She was there, live and waiting to be born, and then..." She stopped for a moment, trying to regain control. There was a reason she didn't talk of this often. The pain—which she'd buried so deep—came raging to the surface and was difficult to control. "Well, I buried them both near the plantation."

"Oh, you poor child," Aunt Dinah murmured.

"No, I'm blessed," Eliza answered, firming her chin. "The Lord saw my pain and He gave me my Harry. I've had him over three years now, and he's my comfort and pride, day and night. But my master went and sold him to a man who meant to take him down the river, to do God knows what, with God knows who."

"But why? Was he disobedient?"

"No, rather Mas'r found that he had to sell some of his hands to pay his debts. He had no choice but to let some of his people go. My son was among them."

Senator Bird turned toward Eliza, tears in his eyes. "How can you say he was good to you, if he did this thing?"

Eliza hung her head, the tears in her own eyes answering those of the senator's. "He did what he had to, sir. I didn't want to believe that he could, but it was the truth. He had no other choice."

"And you ran because you had no other choice," Mrs. Bird finished. "But where will you go?"

"To Canada. My husband also lives on a plantation in Kentucky and will soon escape himself. He plans to run away to Canada. I hope he will meet us there, if he can get away. But I must make it first, on my own. Can you tell me how to get there?" She asked the last question with hope blooming in her heart. Surely they wouldn't turn her in now since they were so sympathetic about Harry.

"Oh child, Canada is a long way off," Mrs. Bird answered quietly. "The journey is dangerous, and if you have catchers after you, it will be even worse. But we'll help you get started, at the very least."

Eliza began to smile at this warmth, but the smile died on her lips when she saw Senator Bird shaking his head.

"We will do no such thing, Mary," he muttered. "You know we cannot."

Mrs. Bird huffed. "Well, if you won't do it, I will. I lost a boy not two months ago—as did you!—and I refuse to let this poor girl suffer the same thing."

He drew up like a rooster about to crow, ready to make his last stand. "The law says—"

"The law is wrong, John!" she interrupted. "And if you're

more politician than Christian, I shall help them without you!"

Senator Bird put a hand on her shoulder, his face firm and set. "I'm a senator, Mary, and I refuse to allow my family to participate in aiding and abetting a known fugitive of the law. That's my final say on the matter. Cudjoe, prepare the carriage. We're taking these runaways to the sheriff."

CHAPTER 23

George ducked farther back into the rotted-out tree trunk, carefully arranging some of the foliage in front of him. The woods behind Maysville were darker than any he'd been in before, but that would serve him well. Now, approaching midnight, there was no one around but for an owl somewhere in the distance and whatever other animals might make their homes here, and he thought he'd be safe for the night. The hollowed-out tree trunk had holes in the middle and at both ends, giving him both a valuable vantage point and three possible points of escape. Although he'd never expected to find a trunk that would hold his large frame, he'd been lucky, and this would make the perfect spot to sit tight until morning.

In short, he could see the world around him, while he lay hidden from anyone else's eyes.

He finished arranging the leaves to his liking and closed his eyes—though not his ears—to get some rest. His plan was to rest here for the night, recover his strength, and set out in the morning. If he got to the docks early enough, he reasoned, he could stow away on a boat and cross the river without notice. Though he knew there were some men in the North who would turn him in to the authorities if they had the chance, it was a free place, and he hoped to travel more easily there.

By the afternoon, he hoped, he'd be well into the Northern territory of Ohio and on his way to freedom.

As his mind began to rest, though, his body began to awaken. Once again he could feel the full force of the whip lashes on his back and the burning of the brand on his palm. Though so much had happened since the whipping, the intensity of the pain reminded him that he had been punished just the night before—had it only been twenty-four hours?—for something that should never have brought repercussions: the ability to use his own will and judgment.

These thoughts and his pains angered him, and his mind raced back to the whipping tree and what had been done to him there. Another man, laying the lash against his back, then pressing an iron into his palm, labeling him property. His right hand curled into a claw around that brand, his heart burning with fury. Until the day he died, that brand would be a reminder of how he'd started his life. He'd cut it out, if he could, or find some way of disguising it.

For it stood for everything that was wrong with the world.

What would Eliza say when she saw it? he wondered suddenly. Would she understand? Would she be as upset and disgusted by it as he was? Would she turn away, afraid to look at the mark that branded him an escaped slave?

No, he thought, pulling his mind away from that idea. Eliza would care for him and try to calm him, as she always did. She would rub ointment into his back, and his hand, and help him heal. She would try to make him laugh, try to make him see that it wasn't the end of the world. That their son—and their future—were more worthy of his thoughts than an abusive white man and his ridiculous laws. He took some comfort in that and felt himself relaxing as he thought about Eliza. Even here and now, out in the wilderness, she was helping him, just with her memory.

Suddenly the night's stillness was broken by the baying of hounds, somewhere in the distance. George's eyes flew open, alarmed at the thought. Dogs—they'd brought dogs! And with hounds...but no, he reasoned. Even if they were hunting him, they didn't have his scent. The dogs might smell him but would assume he was just another person having walked through the woods. They wouldn't follow him.

And if not him, who? he wondered next. The slave catchers wouldn't bring out their dogs unless they had a scent to follow, and if they had a scent, it meant they were chasing some poor man or woman—someone who'd escaped from the plantations down South and was running for freedom. He bit his lip in frustration at that, his mind wandering back to the thoughts he had—and had been having for months now—about the state of the world.

Then his thoughts abruptly turned on him, reminding him quite clearly of the clothing he'd left at the tavern. They did have his scent, he realized with dawning horror. At that moment, his eyes traveled to the left to see one of the dogs he'd heard appearing on the other side of the clearing. The dog's nose dropped to the ground, and he began snuffling through the leaves, seeking the scent he'd been following.

Without wasting a second thought on it, George scooted as quietly as he could toward the opening at the far end of the tree trunk. He scrambled out and was on his feet in moments, flying through the underbrush of the forest. His feet were making too much noise, he knew, but being quiet would mean going slowly and there was no time for that.

He needed to get out of there. Quickly.

He darted through bushes, around trees, and over rocks, jumping and twisting as he came to any obstacles. His eyes had become accustomed to the dark, and he could see the vegetation around him, reaching its branches out to catch at his skin and clothes. Any one of them could offer shelter, but did he dare to stop? Did he dare go up any of the trees? Behind him, he could hear the dogs barking. At least three of them, he thought, though it didn't really matter. There were men with them, shouting along with the dogs, and he was certain that Loker was leading them.

"Get him!" Loker shouted in the distance. "Eat that boy alive! Just leave enough so we can claim the bounty!"

George pushed himself harder at the words. No stopping then, for they meant to set the dogs on him if they caught him. His heart pounded in time to his feet, spelling out both terror and exhilaration. He had a head start on them, but would it be enough?

He pressed on toward the river, hoping to find better hiding places there, or at least get into the water so that the dogs couldn't follow his scent. They were getting closer now—he could hear their calls in the night. As he drew closer to the water, strange shapes began to materialize before him: large floating islands on the water, bobbing with the current and sliding against each other.

"Ice blocks," he muttered, remembering what the men had said during their dinner. He grinned to himself.

If Eliza had done it, then he could do it as well.

He ran harder for the river, his eyes skimming across the water for an ice floe close enough to jump onto. But then he began to think, and he paused. No one could jump across this river without divine intervention. And God had never been on his side. Eliza had been absolutely desperate, with her son at hand, and everyone knew that a mother was virtually invincible when faced with danger to her child. What if he didn't have what it took to get across? What if he didn't make it?

Then, from the corner of his eyes, he saw something. A large Negro man rowing a skiff quite close to the shore. Without thinking, he darted toward it and launched himself into the skiff, landing with a thud. When he looked up, he was surprised to find a Negro man, along with a much older Negro woman, in the skiff. They were both as black as the night, the whites of their eyes showing brightly in the dark, their expressions mirroring the shock of the moment. He sat up, trying to still the rocking of the skiff, and stared at them.

On the bank, the dogs had reached the water—and the end of his trail—and stood barking and howling in frustration.

George glanced at them, terrified, and then laughed and turned back to the couple.

"Thank you for saving my life," he said, his voice rough with running.

Instead of answering immediately, the man reached into his vest and pulled out a gun, turning it on George. "Get off my boat," he snapped.

CHAPTER 24

Eliza glanced down at Harry, laughing. He was dressed in brand-new clothes—a pair of smart trousers, a crisp blue shirt, and suspenders, along with a warm cap. Mrs. Bird had also given him a new, thicker coat, tutting over how cold it was outside. The things had come from the closet of the son the Birds had lost months earlier, and though Eliza felt a bit guilty for taking things that belonged to the dead boy, Mrs. Bird had insisted.

"Better that they find use, and a new life," she said as she gently dressed Harry. "I've kept them for the memory, but it's better if they're useful."

Eliza herself hadn't passed by without anything. Mrs. Bird had taken Eliza promptly into her own room. The room was smaller than the one Mr. and Mrs. Shelby used on the Shelby plantation, but with a larger fireplace. Mrs. Bird had given Eliza one of her own dresses, a new cloak, a bonnet, and a pair of boots. She'd sent Eliza right into the washroom off the master bedroom to dress, and there Eliza had taken advantage of the running water and clean towels. Gazing into the looking glass, she'd seen that she was absolutely filthy, her hair matted and tangled with weeds and even flowers. She'd scrubbed at her face until it shone, then looked into the glass again and studied herself. She looked older already, she thought. Her eyes had a deep sadness that they hadn't before, and she could swear that there were more lines in her cheeks.

Still, she had started on a long, dangerous journey, and that was bound to have changed her. At least she knew what lay at the end of it: her husband, and a free life in Canada. She ducked away from the mirror and began dressing, ready to start the next leg of her journey. The dress was a bit too short and the boots were a shade too large, but she wasn't going to complain. Though not as nice as the dresses she'd left behind at the Shelby plantation, this dress was nice, and she certainly felt cleaner than she had since leaving the Shelbys' home.

All in all, she thought things were starting to look up.

Mrs. Bird nodded in approval when she saw Eliza in the dress and then reached into her closet for a thick cape. "It will keep you warm at night, and it doubles as a blanket if you need it," she said gently, handing it over. "Used to be one of my favorites, but I've a new one now, and you might as well have it."

Eliza took it, somewhat overcome with this show of generosity. "Ma'am, I don't know how I can ever repay you," she whispered, holding the cloak to her chest.

But Mrs. Bird shook her head and shooed her out of the room and back to the kitchen, admonishing her that no thanks were necessary. Before Eliza could protest too much, they were in the kitchen and surrounded by the others again.

"Ready, ma'am?" Cudjoe asked as he strode into the kitchen. "We'd best be going if we're going to make it before anyone comes searching."

She nodded as Cudjoe picked Harry up and followed him out into the courtyard. Cudjoe bundled Harry into the interior of a large carriage, but Eliza turned to the left, to find her new friends Mrs. Bird and Aunt Dinah wiping at their eyes. She rushed toward them and gave them each a hug, thanking the Lord for leading her to this particular house.

"You've both been so kind," she murmured. "I don't know how to thank you."

Mrs. Bird wiped futilely at her eyes. "Now you just get into that carriage and take care of yourself and your boy. I wouldn't have had it any other way. Mr. Bird's all bluster, you know, and he wouldn't have it any other way either."

This brought a laugh from all three women, and Eliza nodded. Although Senator Bird had seemed quite firm in his proclamation, it turned out that his words weren't as final as he'd thought. Mrs. Bird had taken him into another room for a long private discussion, and he'd come back into the kitchen offering to help Eliza and her son in any way that he could. Mrs. Bird had then suggested that Harry and Eliza spend the night, but Senator Bird had—rightly so, in Eliza's opinion—thought this was a bad idea.

"Now Mary, they must be on their way," he'd said. "There's a man after them, and the longer they stay here, the better chance there is that the man will find them. We can't allow that to happen."

"I'm not sure what made him change his mind," Eliza said now, looking deeply into Mrs. Bird's eyes.

"He's a good man. That's why I married him. But even good men let politics cloud their vision, on occasion. He's lucky I'm here to show him the light."

The three women laughed again and then sobered as the senator himself appeared in the doorway.

"Quiet down, you hens, or you'll have the whole neighborhood gossiping," he said. "Come, Eliza, it's time to go."

Eliza ducked down to hug Mrs. Bird one last time. "Thank you so much for everything," she whispered. Then she turned and ran for the carriage where she took Cudjoe's hand and ducked into the contraption. The inside was quite lush, she saw, with velvet on the seats and heavy curtains to keep out the chill. Senator Bird followed her and rapped sharply on the roof of the vehicle, signaling Cudjoe to drive.

"Sir, where are we going?" Eliza asked nervously. She hadn't been a part of the planning and wondered now what this man had in store for her.

"To safety, and that's all you need know," he answered.

She leaned down to massage her sore feet, hoping that wherever they went, it wouldn't necessitate too much walking. The cuts on her feet had been cleaned and bandaged, but using them was going to be painful for some time, regardless of the new boots. Finally she sat back into her seat, pulling Harry against her, and wondered at the senator's answer. He was a reluctant supporter, she knew, and now that it came down to it, she wasn't certain she could trust him. With his wife left behind, he could quite easily go back on his word and take her to the sheriff.

Still, she hoped he wouldn't.

They rode off into the dark, the road beneath them becoming bumpier as they went. Before long, a sudden rainstorm broke over them, and water began to patter on the roof. Senator Bird grumbled in displeasure and pulled open the curtain at the front of the carriage.

"Cudjoe, what's all this?" he asked sharply.

"Rainstorm, sir," Cudjoe answered rather obviously. "Raining like the dickens out here. 'Spect we'll have to stop soon, 'fore the road gets too muddy."

"Well, drive as long as you can," the senator answered. His face drew down into a frown, and Eliza frowned as well. Rain made unpaved roads impassable, and that could last for weeks at a time. What if they got stuck? What if they became stranded?

What if Haley found them before they could get away?

Suddenly there was a large bump, and the carriage came to an abrupt halt, tilting dangerously forward. Harry and Eliza both tumbled from their seat, yelping in surprise. Outside, Cudjoe was shouting.

"Get on, there!" he yelled, presumably at the horses. "Pull harder!" The horses were obviously pulling as hard as they could, though, for she could hear the creaking of their leathers and the huffing of their breath.

Still, the carriage did not move again.

Senator Bird hammered on the ceiling of the carriage. "Cudjoe, what is it now?" he shouted.

The carriage lurched in answer, righting itself with a bounce. But then it kept going, until it was tilted backward. Eliza, Harry, and the senator all found themselves tossed to the side of the carriage, Senator Bird's hat jammed down over his eyes quite unceremoniously. Frightened, Harry began crying.

Outside, Cudjoe continued to shout at the horses, encouraging them to get out of whatever mess they found themselves in.

Eliza, meanwhile, straightened herself and pulled Harry onto her lap, shushing him gently. Within moments, Cudjoe's shouting had died down. Before Eliza could think of what this might mean, the man threw open the door of the carriage.

"Senator, we're stuck in the mud, 'bout to slide down the hill. I'll have to get the rails to get us out."

The senator nearly jumped to his feet. "There's no time to waste, Cudjoe. Let me help." He moved toward the door of the carriage and stepped out, then cussed as he slipped in the mud. Eliza heard the *thwap* of him falling into the sticky earth and stifled a giggle.

A range of bangs and curses followed as the two men retrieved the rails from the top of the carriage and laid them out in front of the wheels, seeking to build a safe ramp for the vehicle. The carriage lurched as both put their shoulders to it, but it refused to move up onto the rails.

Suddenly the senator appeared at the door.

"Eliza, would you and Harry step out? If we lighten the load, perhaps we can get this damned contraption to move."

Eliza nodded, murmuring her agreement, and stepped out into the pouring rain, covering Harry's head as best she could with her hands and cloak. The world around them was quite dark, but she got away from the carriage, to what she presumed was a safe distance, and watched as the men heaved away. They were making very little progress, though, and gave up before long.

"Well Eliza, you may as well get back into the carriage," Senator Bird said, wiping at his face. "We can't move it. I'm sending Cudjoe with one of the horses for help."

Eliza glanced from the senator's face to Cudjoe's, suddenly worried. This was the very thing she'd feared—stuck on the side of the road with no hope of escape, and Haley getting closer with every passing minute. They'd already lost so much time, and now they would lose more as Cudjoe rode back to town for help.

At this rate, Haley would be on them sooner rather than later. She couldn't allow that to happen.

"I'll help," she said, kissing Harry and then putting him down. "Perhaps a third person will make the difference."

The two men laughed, looked up and down her small frame, and shook their heads.

"That boy's the heaviest thing you've ever lifted, I'll warrant!" Cudjoe sputtered.

"Yes, but you must let me try," she answered desperately. "We can't wait here. There's a man after us!"

"Well then, great ice river jumper, let's see what you can do," the senator agreed, moving to stand behind the carriage again. Cudjoe put his shoulder to the carriage beside the senator, and Eliza moved to push next to them.

"On the count of three, people," the senator huffed. "One, two, three..."

At the count, they all threw their weight into the carriage, pushing with all their might against the slick mud underneath them. The carriage rocked, then moved forward a couple of inches, but slid back as soon as they stopped pushing.

"There now, I told you," Cudjoe muttered.

Eliza looked at Harry and, taking courage from his small form, quoted, "Matthew 17:20. 'If ye have faith as a grain of mustard seed, ye shall say unto this mountain, remove hence to yonder place; and it shall remove; and nothing shall be impossible for you.' Again!" And, without waiting for a response, she shoved against the carriage again, desperate for it to move this time.

The two men joined her and heaved, pushing against the carriage with their combined strength. Ahead of the carriage the horses pulled, adding their weight to the attempt. Eliza prayed with all her might, begging her Lord to watch over her now and help her escape this new threat. And quite suddenly, and with a great sucking sound, the carriage came free, rumbling up onto the railings and sliding onto the road.

Eliza stood, her heart hammering with the effort, and dusted her hands off. "Now," she said calmly, "I think we can go."

CHAPTER 25

George stared down the barrel of the gun, shocked speechless. The man—not so speechless—continued to wave the gun toward George, indicating that this new stowaway should exit the vessel immediately.

"I said get off my boat," he said, his voice low and threatening.

The sky broke above them, and George looked up, taking in the storm clouds above them and the sudden rainstorm. He looked back down to the man, taking in his broad features and deep, intense eyes. "What?" he asked softly.

"We don't have anyone chasin' us," the man responded. "But you seem to have the entire state of Kentucky after you. You're goin' to get us all caught, and I won't have it. Now get. Off. My boat."

George sputtered. This man was throwing him out? With slave catchers on the shore, waiting for him? In the pouring rain? How could he?

"Jim, how could you?" the woman asked, echoing George's own thoughts, and he turned to her thankfully.

The man, though, scowled more firmly. "I'm thinkin' it's better he get caught on his own than the three of us get caught together."

The woman scowled powerfully enough to compete fairly with the man, and George suppressed an unwilling smile, a bit relieved that he didn't have to fight this particular battle for himself.

"Put that gun down and start rowin', and I guarantee we'll all three get away just fine," the woman muttered.

Jim huffed but didn't seem willing to give up the fight. "Get out!" he muttered, staring at George once again.

"Jim!" the woman snapped.

Jim heaved a great sigh, expanding a chest that was fully twice as large as George's, and gave in with fairly good grace. "Well then," he said quickly, "if you're goin' to stay, least you could do is row." He handed both oars to George, who put them quickly into the water, agreeing wholeheartedly with the woman's assessment of the situation.

"Thank you kindly for your compassion, ma'am," he told her.

"Well now, can't leave one of our own out there to the dogs," she answered, sitting back placidly. "Name's Anita Donald, and this is my son James."

"I'm George Harris. Thank you again for savin' me. I was...well..."

"Out of options, and we've all been there," she answered kindly. "Just thank the good Lord above that we saw you. They would've caught you if we hadn't been there."

George looked back at the bank. The dogs were still prowling the water, looking for a way to come after the boat. Three figures had joined them now—Haley, Loker, and Marks, he thought, coming quickly out of the forest and squinting through the rain to point toward the small boat.

"We'll be comin' after you, boy, and don't you forget it!" Loker yelled, furious at George's escape. "We'll see you soon!"

"You'll never catch me, Loker!" George shouted back, full of confidence after the escape.

Then George heard two gunshots, and bullets threw up splashes of water around the skiff.

Anita screamed in fright.

"Stop talkin', boy, and get to rowin', or they're goin' to catch us right now!" Jim snapped.

George nodded and put his back into the rowing, pulling the boat farther and farther from the shore while Jim used a third oar to steer around and through the ice floes. With each passing iceberg, George's heart lifted. Escaped. Those men had been after him and he'd escaped. For the first time, his status as a newly free man seemed real, and his heart sang.

He glanced at the other two people in the skiff, though, and frowned. The woman seemed kind enough, but the man hadn't wanted to bring him, and he wasn't certain that he could trust either one of them. They seemed to have escaped themselves, but they could just as easily turn him in to the authorities and take the reward money. It was a chance George couldn't afford to take. Eliza and Harry were depending on him, wherever they were. He didn't know how far Eliza had gone, but he knew that she'd crossed the river. She was a house maid, though, and a spoiled woman, all told. He didn't think she'd make it all the way to Canada on her own. He had to find her before it was too late.

Even if it meant leaving his two saviors as soon as they hit shore.

CHAPTER 26

Much later, after a long and bumpy road, the carriage emerged from the night in front of a large farmhouse. Eliza glanced out the window, wondering where they were. The house was large and rambling—like many farmhouses—but almost completely dark, with a barn standing tall behind it, and the trees leaning over it as though providing shelter. It certainly didn't look like a welcoming place, and she wondered again what the senator was actually going to do with her.

At the noise of their arrival, the master of the house—or so it seemed—appeared at the door. He was tall and bristling with whiskers against the light of the house, but he looked respectable, from what Eliza could see, about as tall as George's six-foot frame and dressed in a red flannel hunting shirt and trousers. He had heavy, greying blond hair, which was mussed as though he'd just been in bed, and he held a candle aloft, blinking sleepily.

Senator Bird got out of the carriage with a grunt and gestured for Eliza to follow him. Then he walked with little hesitation up to the man in the doorway.

"Hello, John," Senator Bird said.

"Well hello, John," the other man answered quietly.

"That's Senator John now, you know," Senator Bird answered.

"Well then, Senator John, how can I help you?"

"Are you a man that will shelter a poor woman and child from slave catchers?" the senator asked boldly.

Eliza caught her breath. Surely this was a way to get caught, advertising their situation like that. The man in the doorway turned to glance at her, though, and she could see that his eyes were full of kindness. She thought this man would help her, if given the chance.

But he shook his head. "Heard tell that you voted for the new Fugitive Slave Act, John Bird. Is this a trap?"

"No no, this isn't a trap. Tell me, John, how long have you known me?"

"Too long," the man answered with a chuckle.

"And have you ever known me to be dishonest?" the senator continued.

"Not yet."

"I brought this woman to you because I hope you can help her and her boy. Her name is Eliza, and this is little Harry. Eliza, this is John Van Trompe. He, like you, is from Kentucky."

The man nodded. "I was once a considerable land owner there, in fact."

Eliza gasped. A land owner in Kentucky! Then he'd owned slaves! "Why have you brought me here?" she snapped, wondering what game the senator was playing. Had he brought her here to try to turn her over to another master? "I thought I could trust you!"

The man named John Van Trompe held up his hands in a conciliatory gesture. "Now calm down, miss. I realized the error of my ways. Found the Lord, freed my slaves, and now I help others find their freedom as well. I suppose you've heard of the Underground Railroad?"

Eliza, unable to answer, nodded. She didn't trust him yet, but why would he ask her about the Underground Railroad if he meant to turn her in to the authorities or send her home? Was he trying to trick her into admitting something?

"I ask again, sir, are you a man that will shelter a poor woman and her son from the slave catchers?" the senator asked suddenly.

Van Trompe nodded once. "I am."

Eliza's heart rose up into her throat at that simple statement. He was going to shelter them. Help them on their road to Canada. She could have hugged him right then, but the senator had more information to pass on.

"A man named Haley is searching for them. He may have brought others. We don't know how far back they are."

Van Trompe stretched his tall frame and laughed. "Well, if they come for her, we'll be ready. I've got seven sons, each six feet tall, and we'll stand between her and the slave catchers if we must. Come in, come in."

The senator stepped into the house, chuckling softly to himself, but Eliza turned and stared out into the night. Somewhere out there, Haley was searching for her. How close was he? Would he find her here?

Just then, she felt a gentle hand on her arm. "Now girl, you needn't be afraid. I've got protection for us." Van Trompe gestured toward the walls of his house, and Eliza turned to see a number of guns on their racks. "Most people know that it would be unwise to try to get into my house when I'm in it," he added with a laugh.

Eliza nodded and stepped across the doorstep, feeling as though she was in a safe place once again. And now, finally, on their way to Canada. She hoped that Uncle Tom had gotten word to George, as he'd promised, and that her husband would find a way to meet them there. She needed him now more than ever.

Eliza made her way into the room Van Trompe had opened for her and put Harry down softly on the bed. Instead of lying down herself, however, she turned back to the closed door and ducked down, putting her ear against the keyhole. She was with friends, she thought, but her instincts told her not to trust anyone completely. She wanted to know what these men were up to.

"She's handsome, John," Van Trompe was saying.

"Yes, and typically the handsome ones have the best reasons to run," the senator replied sadly. "Thank you for helping them."

"Anything for the innocent. I'll get them to the next station, and from there they'll go on to Canada. If they're lucky."

"Lucky?"

"Not everyone makes it, John. But we'll do our best to get them there."

She heard a long, tired sigh from the senator. "Well, that's better than I could do for them. Good night, John."

"Good night, John."

"That's Senator John, to you."

The tall man laughed. "Yes of course, how could I forget?"

Eliza heard the door close then and moved back to the bed, exhausted by her long ordeal and this constant state of depending on strangers. She hoped they'd be in Canada soon, safely away from the dangers of this nation.

CHAPTER 27

George put his back into the rowing, hoping to get to the other side of the river as quickly as possible so that he might continue his journey. He wasn't certain yet how he was going to get away from Jim—who still held a pistol aimed at him—but he was positive that he must. If Jim planned to turn him in to the authorities, he couldn't stay, and he would move more quickly without the old woman, as sweet as she was.

"Watch out!" Jim muttered for the fifth time in as many minutes, motioning toward another piece of ice. He stuck his oar into the water and used it to guide the skiff around the ice floe as George provided the propulsion.

They navigated through several more floes of ice and came finally to the other bank of the Ohio River. As the skiff ran aground, its bottom scraping against the stones and dirt of the shore, George allowed himself a quick grin. Free territory. On this side of the river, he knew, white men didn't own Negroes. Although he might not find fair treatment here—he was, after all, still a Negro—at least he was free.

And that alone meant the world to him.

"Stop dreamin', and help me get the skiff up on dry land," Jim snapped after hopping out of the boat himself and helping Anita carefully to shore.

George nodded, drawing his attention back to the real world, and disembarked himself, leaning to drag the boat up onto the dirt. Then he turned and followed Jim and Anita as they crept along the bank, keeping to the deepest shadows under the foliage. The trees seemed taller here, he thought, as if they were reaching up for the sky. Refusing to provide as much cover for those trying to hide underneath. It made him jumpy. Less secure. Suddenly Jim dropped to his knees, his eyes going wide, and put a finger up to his lips.

"We're not alone," he whispered.

George knelt as well, his heart racing, and looked into the woods to see a Negro man and woman creeping along. The woman carried a child, who had obviously been crying, and both man and woman looked as though they were about to drop from fright. The man, though, had a determination about him that indicated his stubborn belief in what they were doing. He was taking his family to freedom, and nothing was going to stop him.

George breathed out slowly. Why, it could have been him with Eliza and Harry.

"Runaways," Jim murmured, easing his posture somewhat.

"How do you know?" George asked, though he could see that they were running as well as any other man.

"Not walkin' like free people," Jim answered. "And look at their dress. That's slave dress. And who else but slaves would be carryin' a baby about at this hour?"

George nodded. It had to be after midnight, he knew that much, and Jim was right—no decent people would be out creeping around the river right now. During the summer, perhaps—lovers out to have a midnight picnic. But not a family. Not in this weather. The man and woman must have heard something then, for they broke into a run, spilling out onto the shore from the tree line. Two white men followed them out of the trees, shouting, and George, Jim, and Anita ducked farther back into the bushes.

"Slave catchers," Jim said grimly, echoing George's unspoken thought.

"But Ohio is a free state," George answered, voicing his

other thought. Why would there be slave catchers here, where black men were allowed to walk free?

Jim shook his head slowly, then cast a long glance at his mother. George watched, wondering what exactly that look was for, but then Jim turned toward him and answered. "Only if you were born free, or set free on purpose and have the papers to prove it. If you're runnin', they can chase you through any state they want. Only safe places are Canada and the grave."

George watched the family running down the shore and saw that the white men were gaining on them. He knew immediately what he had to do. "We must help them," he said firmly, rising. "We have a pistol. We can't let them be captured."

"I have the pistol, and we've already helped more people than I like," Jim answered shortly. "We stay here. Out of sight. Out of trouble."

George stood up taller. "Then I'll help them myself. I'm no coward."

Jim turned his pistol quickly on George, pushing it against his chest. "No, you will not. If you help them, you'll reveal our hiding place. Already told you how I feel 'bout you gettin' us caught."

"You'd shoot me for trying to help them?"

Jim scoffed. "I'll shoot you for bein' stupid, especially if it gets those slave catchers after us! You think you're bein' brave, but it's stupidity to try to help anyone else. Few hours ago you couldn't help yourself. Now you want to risk your own life helpin' someone else. Those slave catchers have got more guns than you, and friends and dogs as well. They'll catch the family, and if you're tryin' to help them, they'll catch you as well."

George scowled, frustrated. "So I should do nothin', like you?"

Jim took a deep breath, and for the first time his broad features softened. "I'm tryin' to get my mother to Canada, see her safe. I have a home there. I'd like to see her livin' the life of a free woman. Would you risk your own mother's life for someone you didn't know?"

George shut his mouth then. No, he wouldn't have risked his mother for people he didn't know. If he'd been in that position, with Eliza or Harry with him, perhaps, he would have done the same as Jim. Still...he turned back to the shore, noting that the slave catchers had caught up to the family and were pushing them rather roughly back into the woods. The man fell to his knees, and one of the catchers set about him with a stick, beating the poor man until he cried out. The woman shrieked, which set the child to crying, and soon the whole group was making so much noise that he thought he and his friends were going to have to move, just to get away from it. But still the slave catcher hit the poor man on the ground, taunting him about having thought that he could get away from him. Taunting him for daring to think that he deserved to be free.

George watched, his eyes filling with tears over the situation, and felt his determination hardening, growing stronger. Those people were so similar to his own family, and he couldn't help but be sympathetic to them. He would have helped them if he could. But now that they were captured...

"When I'm a free man, and set up in Canada with my family, I'll return to the States. Help those that I can't help now," he vowed quietly, more to himself than anyone else. "I won't allow this to happen anymore. It's not right. No man has a right to abuse another man so, and I'll take my people away. Away to where they'll be safe. And free."

"Well then, I suggest you get to Canada and get to work," Jim answered kindly, one hand on George's shoulder.

George turned to him, recognizing now that the man might be a friend after all. "You said you live in Canada?" he asked.

Jim pushed out his lips and nodded in confirmation. "Ran away over a year ago, found my way north and over the border. Have a house and carpentry shop in Montreal. And I mean to get back to them with my mother."

"Why did you come back?" George asked, though the reason was clear. He'd come back for Anita.

"Always meant to come back for Ma, but had to come back somewhat earlier than I planned. Heard Mas'r Donald was punishin' her for me runnin' away. As if she'd helped me, or somethin' like that."

Anita nodded. "Jim here was the highest-earnin' slave on the plantation. Mas'r Donald didn't like losin' him. Spent years teachin' him carpentry, trainin' him up to be the best in the county. Made lots of money off the neighbors bringin' their orders to the plantation, have Jim make their furniture for 'em. Made him furious when Jim ran."

George nodded. Much the same story as his own. And if Jim lived in Canada… "Do you know the way to get there?" he asked breathlessly. "Canada, I mean."

"I do."

"Will you take me with you? Help me find my family?"

"No! We've already saved you once."

"Jim!" Anita snapped.

Jim drew his lips into a thin line, thinking, then nodded once. "You can come. But the minute you put us in danger, we're finished."

CHAPTER 28

After the slave catchers had dragged the man up to his feet and hustled the family back into the woods— back to whatever grim life awaited them down South—Jim declared their party safe to move again. "Those men won't be back for anythin' else," he said shortly. "They got their bounty."

George, still painfully aware that he'd let that family be captured and feeling responsible for their fate, sighed deeply. One shove from Jim, though, and he turned back toward the future. "Well then, where're we goin'?" he asked, glaring into the darkness of the woods around them.

"Little place called Ripley," Jim said wisely. "Big town, full of people that don't get in your way. Everyone minds their own business. Makes it the perfect place for us."

George didn't answer, thinking that the town did indeed

sound like the right sort of place for a party such as theirs but wondering exactly what Jim had in mind. He'd said that he would take George with them into Canada but that hadn't answered George's entire question. He was, after all, still missing his family, though he had no idea where they might be. As they walked, he tried to put himself in Eliza's shoes and figure out where she might have gone or how she meant to get to Canada, for he had no doubt that she was heading to the North. She knew he'd find them there, and surely that was her goal. But how would she get there?

In the end, he decided that he wouldn't be able to find her on his own. Besides, if Jim and Anita were heading north and Eliza was taking Harry north as well, in the end, surely their paths would cross. There were only a few ways for Negroes to travel in this country, even in the free North, and perhaps he could find someone who'd seen her. The thought gave him comfort, and by the time they reached Ripley, he was feeling more optimistic than he had since leaving the factory.

Upon coming to the outskirts of Ripley, Jim turned smartly to the left and passed the town, going instead up a large hill at its borders. Anita, who was obviously past her prime, struggled with the hill, and before long Jim ducked down to lift her in his arms, using his long legs to stride quickly up the slope. George hurried after him, wondering anew where they were headed.

At the top of the hill, they found a large house painted a sedate blue color with white trim, and all its shutters closed. Wide open fields stretched out around the place, and George could see that whoever lived here made their living as a farmer. The front door to the house was closed, however, and George looked closely at it, frowning.

"Looks deserted," he observed quietly.

Jim shook his head. "Belongs to the Reverend John Rankin," he answered, frowning as well. "Active abolitionist 'round here."

At the word, George's mind cleared. If there was an abolitionist in the area, then this was exactly where they needed to be. "Well then, let's go," he said, starting toward the house.

Jim stopped him with a hand on his arm. "Not that way. 'Round there." He pointed to the side of the house where George could see a smaller door. "If we were welcome, we'd see that door open, with a candle burning in the window next to it."

George looked at the smaller door, which was closed, and then up toward the windows, which were all shut and darkened. "Well, this isn't the right place, then. Is there another home? Somewhere else we can go?"

Jim shook his head, looking quite worried. "Rankin is the most active abolitionist in this town. If his doors are closed, it means it's not safe to be in his home. And if it's not safe to be in his home, then it's not safe for us to be in this town. Somethin's changed here. We'd best be goin'."

"Goin'? But you said—"

"Only one thing would close Rankin's house, George, and that's slave catchers in the area," Jim said, cutting him off. "Patrollers or slave catchers have been here, and if they know about the house, then they're watchin' the house. We saw some of them down by the river, maybe. Just bein' here brings danger on us and the Rankin household."

George bit his lip. That he understood. And if this man was helping people like George, the last thing he wanted was to bring trouble on his house. Still, he thought, there must have been some sort of backup plan. "What now?"

"We have to find our own way onto the Underground Railroad," Jim answered firmly. "We're goin' to need a horse and carriage."

"And where do you think we're goin' to get that?" George

asked, his mind spinning. Find their own way? As if it was just as simple as that?

"We'll borrow it," the larger man said abruptly, moving back the way they'd come.

"You mean steal," George snapped back. He held out his hand for Anita and began to follow Jim, who whirled around, his face angry.

"Don't get righteous with me. The way I see it, you stole yourself from your master, same as I did, so we're already guilty. Went down and stole my mother as well, and far as I can tell, you took it upon yourself to encourage your wife to run. We're all criminals here, George, and if you want to get to Canada, this is the way it has to be. I'm takin' my mother, and we're goin'. You don't like it—you can find your own way."

George paused. Eliza and Harry were out there somewhere, hopefully on the Underground Railroad already. And as far as he knew, Jim was his only way to follow them, even if the plan was lacking in originality. "Let's go borrow that horse and carriage then," he said decidedly. He needed to find his family, and this was the only way to do it.

So back down the hill they went, searching for houses that looked prosperous enough to host a horse and carriage. At the bottom of the hill and back in the forest, Jim motioned for his mother to sit on a fallen log and wait for them, then struck back out into the open, his head swiveling from left to right in search of a likely house.

When they came to a row of houses that looked richer than the others, they began searching barns. While some residents had horses, few had carriages, and while others had carriages, they were lacking horses. A few of the barns had large locks on their doors, keeping Jim and George out completely.

"This search isn't very strategic," George observed after their fourth failed search.

"Quiet, before you wake the town!" Jim snapped. "This next house is the one. I can feel it."

George snorted, thinking that guessing at houses and "feeling" that they would have horses or carriages wasn't very strategic either. "It better be. The sun will be risin' soon, and then there won't be any more searchin.'"

They walked through the front gate of the next house and strolled toward the barn, taking care to keep their footsteps quiet. When they opened the doors, they found—to George's shocked pleasure—both a carriage and horse inside and worked together to roll the carriage out into the driveway.

"Now the horse," Jim whispered. He walked back into the barn and opened the stall door, then grabbed at the horse's halter. He jerked and yanked, trying to lead the horse out into the aisle as quickly as possible.

Jim was evidently not a natural horseman though, for the horse refused to budge.

Jim pulled harder, and the horse grew heavier, standing even more firmly in place. Then it began to struggle, snorting and pawing at the ground in protest. George watched, torn between amusement and frustration, and finally walked toward the pair, thinking that he'd best handle this particular situation if he wanted to get out of there before the sun rose.

He took the struggling horse from Jim, then put a hand to its nose and spoke quietly to it. It didn't matter what he said, he knew, as long as his voice was low and comforting. Horses liked the sound of a human voice. It made them feel safe. Gradually, the horse settled, eyeing Jim with distrust but holding steady under George's hand.

"Leave that devil animal here!" Jim snarled. "It's goin' to give away our position."

"Nonsense," George responded. "I've been handlin' horses since I was young. Easier to get them to work for you if you're kind to them. Though watchin' your performance, I wonder if you've ever handled one at all." He glanced sideways at Jim, saw that the man was growing angrier, and turned back to the horse.

"Easy there," he murmured. "Sorry for our friend Jim's behavior. He just doesn't know any better. He's worried about his mother, who we left in the woods. And I'm worried about my family, who are out there on their own. We need your help. If you'll take us away from this place, I'll make sure that you find a home when we land wherever we're goin'."

Jim laughed. "So now you speak horse?"

"No, but I know how it feels to be mistreated or abandoned." George led the horse—now fully willing—out to the carriage and proceeded to strap him into the harness, taking his time with the buckles to make sure that they didn't rub the wrong way and thanking the horse for his willingness. Jim followed, his face beginning to show a grudging respect.

"Well then, bringin' you with us may not have been a mistake after all. Let's get my mother and go. I just hope the patrollers haven't found her yet."

CHAPTER 29

George, Jim, and Anita had been crowded together under the scant canopy of the carriage, driving through the still-driving rain, for over an hour by the time the sun began to rise. At that point, Jim declared the main roads no longer safe for them. They pulled into a dusty, deserted lane and followed it through the thinning tree cover to an abandoned barn some ways from the road. The place obviously hadn't seen human habitation for some time —the paint was worn off the fence, and the barn itself looked as though it had lost half of its roof. Behind sat a house, which was in even worse shape, two walls having fallen in. Jim declared that it was the perfect place to hide, certainly not belonging to anyone else, and pulled into the barn. He jumped down from the driver's seat and went immediately to the door with his pistol to watch in case anyone had seen them. George and Anita, less concerned about pursuit—they hadn't seen anyone on the road, after all—set about clearing some of the rubble from the floor. George pushed old, molded hay and straw out to the walls, then turned back to help Anita with a rusted-out piece of machinery. Once they had a large enough clearing, they laid out the rugs and blankets they'd found in the carriage.

"Jim, wake me in an hour," George told the man firmly. "We all need sleep, but you and I will take turns keepin' watch."

Jim nodded once, then turned tensely back to the door. George and Anita lay down on the rugs and began to talk to pass the time.

"Tell me about your family, George," Anita murmured, her eyes heavy. "You're goin' after them, figure they must be somethin' special. What's your wife's name? How did you meet her?"

George smiled and began telling her about Eliza and Harry. How he'd met Eliza on one of her trips into town for her mistress, fallen madly in love, and begun courting her. How he'd followed her around like a lovesick puppy dog for six months before she finally consented to his attentions. And how they'd married before a reverend and her master and mistress. How, a couple of years later, Harry had come while George himself was working at the factory. Before he knew it, his eyes were growing heavy, and he was asleep.

~

They were back on the road at sundown, having spent the day in the barn together, taking turns sleeping, standing guard, and talking about their pasts. George had told the others all about his family, and Jim had regaled George and Anita with stories of his new life in Canada. By the time they got back on the road, George was starting to feel as though these people were his friends, rather than just traveling companions.

The night around them grew dark quickly—better cover, Jim noted—and the temperature dropped almost as fast as night. An hour into their journey, Anita crawled into the back of the carriage and brought back the blankets for them to use against the night cold. George gathered one of the rugs around him and gazed into the distance. He could see mountains there, with snow along their caps, and wondered how long it would be until they were there. They'd have to cross those mountains to get to Canada, he thought. Would they survive the trip? Would they freeze to death, or make it to the other side, and their freedom?

He sent up a prayer—to a God he wasn't sure he believed in —that wherever Eliza and Harry were, they were warm enough, and safe, with plenty of food and a large fireplace in front of them.

Then he sent up another prayer that he would find them soon so that they could go on together. He missed them powerfully, and found himself wondering more and more often when he would find them again.

After several hours of driving—George and Jim still talking about their pasts and the future—Jim pulled in at an unremarkable house and slowed the horse.

"Where are we?" George asked, confused. He gazed intently at the house and its surrounding buildings, but he didn't see any markings that indicated inhabitation—or help.

"The home of a good friend," Jim replied mysteriously.

George frowned. "Another friend? The last friend you took us to had closed his house. Think there are slave catchers here too?"

"I have no idea," Jim answered. "No more questions. Ma will stay here while we go see about the house. And George, try to walk like a free man, rather than someone who constantly expects to be caught."

George pushed out his chest, affronted at this speech. "What's that supposed to mean?"

"Only that you've been walkin' like a slave afraid of bein' caught by the dogs. Stooped over, constantly lookin' over your shoulder, like you think the catchers might appear at any moment. Walk like a man who's free and proud and you'll draw less attention to yourself," Jim answered, smiling.

"Why?"

"Even in the dark, people might be watchin' this house. They see you walkin' like a runaway..."

"They'll know I'm a runaway," George finished, seeing exactly where Jim was going with his speech.

Jim nodded, satisfied, and walked toward the house, leaving George to follow along. He knocked once at the door and waited for a moment. When no one answered, he knocked again.

Suddenly the door flew open, the muzzle of a shotgun emerging. Farther back in the house, George could hear the sound of the gun being cocked.

A tall, rough-looking white man appeared on the other end of the gun, scowling powerfully, his beard and hair both fairly bristling with aggression. "What business do you have here?" he asked sharply.

Jim made calming motions with his hands. "Calm down, friend."

"Everything will be plenty calm once I've shot you both. Now who are you?"

"I'm James Donald, from Kentucky. We met last year."

The man snorted. "It can't be."

"Van Trompe, it's me. I came back for my mother, and I need your help again."

"A likely story. I think you're probably a trap, is what you are. Now stand still or your next move will be your last."

George tried to shrink back into the shadows without moving. He hoped this Van Trompe person hadn't seen him, though he doubted it. He didn't know who this man was, or why Jim had called him friend, but he seemed less than friendly now. The man stepped back into the house and appeared a moment later with a candle, which he passed under George's face and then turned on Jim.

"My God!" he muttered, shocked. "It is you, Jim Donald. I'd recognize those broad features anywhere! How did you get here? I'd heard that the conductors in Ripley closed the station there."

Jim grinned. "They did. Had to borrow a carriage and get here on our own."

Van Trompe grinned back and turned toward George, looking him up and down. "And who's this?"

"This is George. Ma and I picked him up at the river. He was...havin' some trouble there."

The man grunted again. "Your name George Harris, boy?" he asked.

George jumped at hearing his full name, surprised. "Yes, I am. How do you know my name?"

Van Trompe laughed. "Heard it twice today. Once from your wife and then again from some slave catchers that came after her."

George's heart stopped. "Eliza?" he murmured. "You've seen Eliza?"

"Came here last night, courtesy of a friend of mine," Van Trompe answered briskly. "Another unexpected Railroad passenger. I gave her and your son food and a place to rest, then sent them on to the next stop."

"She's alive?" George breathed. "And safe? Is she well?"

"Far as I know. Got her out of here just in time, matter of fact. Got home to find three slave catchers in my yard."

George's heart hardened again. They were here already? "And their names?" he asked, already knowing the answer.

"One was named Haley, big one was named Loker. Never got introduced to the little one."

"You send them away?" Jim asked, looking around fearfully. Was this a trap after all? Had this man teamed up with the slave catchers, in case George came after his family?

Van Trompe nodded, his mouth firm and disapproving. "'Course I did. Told them I'd never seen any slaves in this part of the county, much less slaves that stopped to give names like George, Eliza, and Harry Harris. They tried to tell me that they had a legal right to search the property, seeing as how they were looking for runaways."

"And?" George asked, wondering at the truth of this story.

"Told them if they stepped into my home, I'd shoot them all dead. And then their ghosts could report me to the sheriff," Van Trompe answered with a bark of laughter.

Jim laughed as well. "I take it they declined."

"The big fellow, Loker, wanted to test me, but the little one said they shouldn't. He was the brains of the operation, if you ask me."

"Can you take me to my family?" George asked suddenly, jumping to the thought foremost in his mind. If this man knew where Eliza and Harry had gone, perhaps he could tell George. Within hours, perhaps he could be with his family again.

"Sure I can take you in that direction, but we'd best take some time to prepare," Van Trompe answered. "Figure you folks have been on the road for some time, and you're probably hungry. Wet, without a doubt, given the weather." He ducked under the eaves of his house and looked up at the sky, his expression thoughtful. A drop fell from the roof, narrowly missing his face, and he drew back again, shaking his head. "And we need to prepare for a fight on the road. Those slave catchers couldn't get into my house, but they came here looking, and that means they think I have you and your family. Guess my reputation is getting larger than I realized. They'll be waiting up the road, thinking I'll take you to the next stop."

"I have a pistol," Jim answered quickly.

"Good! But, you're going to need more than that," Van Trompe answered. He stood to the side and pointed to a wall full of guns, grinning. "But the good Lord always provides."

George glanced from the guns back to the man in front of them, wondering at this man. Jim had said he was a friend, but what kind of white man kept that many guns, unless for hunting? Further, what kind of white man put his own life in danger to help runaway slaves? By his own words, this man had helped Eliza and Harry escape and was willing to do the same for George, Jim, and Anita. Something felt wrong there. Distrustful.

George stepped into the house, though, telling himself that he was being paranoid. This man had helped Eliza and Harry, after all, and he'd helped Jim on his way to Canada the year before. Jim knew him and trusted him, and Jim hadn't done anything to prove himself false.

Besides, Van Trompe knew where Eliza and Harry were. As far as George was concerned, that was the most important knowledge anyone could have at the moment. He walked deeper into the dark hallway, smelling wood smoke and a recently cooked ham. Food. Warmth. Protection. Yes, he'd use this man to find his family, and then proceed to Canada.

CHAPTER 30

Eliza gazed around the small farmhouse, quite surprised at the turn of events. In just two days, she'd gone from despair over Harry's impending sale, to running through the wilderness on her own, to jumping a river of ice and finding a kind stranger—and then another, and then another—to sitting in a small, cozy kitchen with a family that felt almost like her own.

Van Trompe had brought her here, to the home of the Hallidays, in the last darkness of the night, promising her that the family would treat her and her son as their own and see her on her journey. She'd rarely been so surprised at the behavior of a group of people. The lady of the house—one Rachel Halliday—had indeed made her immediately welcome, setting out tea and cakes for Eliza and Harry and stoking the fire brighter to warm their limbs. She sat now with Eliza while the oldest girl, Mary, fed Harry his breakfast. Around them, she saw that the kitchen was as bright and cheerful a place as she'd ever been. The walls were a sunny yellow color while the furniture—sturdy stuff, and homemade, she could swear—was of dark, solid wood, with some whitewash for color. The family had one of the largest stoves Eliza had ever seen, and Rachel had told her that she and two other women cooked for the entire colony on special occasions.

What was more, though, their warmth and good cheer gave the place a safe, cozy feeling. She'd met several of the family, and they had—whether man or woman—been kind and gentle with her and Harry, making certain that they were comfortable and satisfied.

"I don't know how I can thank you," Eliza murmured for the third or fourth time. "You're saving our lives."

"Simply doing God's work," Rachel answered, adjusting the lace cap on her curls.

Eliza nodded, having been told that this was a family of Quakers who thought of themselves as God's people. They lived a simple life and did all they could to act as the Lord would have them act. It was a philosophy she could identify with, and she'd felt an immediate warming to people who lived their lives that way.

"You and Harry can stay here as long as you wish," Rachel continued. "And we hope you'll stay for some time."

"Oh, but we can't," Eliza gasped, pulled from her reverie. "There's a man after my little boy, and I must get to Canada as soon as possible."

"I've been told about the men after you, but we can offer protection," Rachel answered firmly. "Is your husband in Canada then?"

"He's in Kentucky," Eliza answered sadly. "But he's bein' sorely mistreated there, and I expect he'll leave soon and make his way to Canada himself. I hope to meet him there."

"And what will you do until he arrives? Or if you can't find him? Canada is a large place, you know, and the chances of you finding each other slim. You must find shelter, and a job of your own, so that you can care for yourself and your little one. What will you do if he never comes?"

Eliza shook her head. The thought had never entered her mind. She was certain that George would come for her and had never doubted it. But the idea that they might get to Canada before he did and have to take care of themselves... "I'll find a way to provide for us until he comes. He won't desert us," she said confidently. She didn't even give thought to the idea that they might not find each other. That possibility was too terrible to contemplate—particularly now, when she felt safe for the first time in days.

Rachel looked narrowly at Eliza, her expression one of worry and some sympathy. "What did you do on the plantation? What are your skills?"

"I took care of the mistress. Dressed her hair, helped her choose her clothes, got her the things she required..."

Rachel sat back, a slight frown on her face. "So you don't have any skills? Most slaves that come through here have skills—a way to make a living in the North."

"Oh, I have skills," Eliza exclaimed, suddenly understanding what Rachel meant. "I've been a seamstress my whole life, and Missis Shelby brought me up to it. Made all her dresses, I did, except those that she bought in town. I can do that in Canada as well, surely. Women must need dresses there. Don't they?"

Just then, Rachel's husband, Simeon Halliday, walked through the door, his great black coat billowing behind him. Eliza gazed up at him, with his flowing mustaches and dark, kind eyes. He was a good man, she was sure, and caring. He would set them safely on the road to Canada. And if George came after them, she hoped Simeon would tell him where they'd gone and how to find them.

"How are you, Eliza?" he asked.

"Well, thank you," she replied, wondering why he would ask. Surely he didn't expect anything to have happened in the past few hours to have changed that?

Simeon nodded and turned to his wife. "Mother, will you join me in the living room for a moment?"

Rachel glanced at him, her face confused, then rose and walked into the other room with him. Eliza watched her, frightened at this secrecy. What did Simeon have to say that she couldn't hear? Was he telling Rachel that Eliza and Harry had to leave the house? Or worse—that the slave catchers were on their way here, to take Eliza and her son back? Suddenly her heart was hammering away in her chest, all the most terrible possibilities flying through her mind. She'd thought she was safe, but what if she'd been wrong?

A moment later, Rachel reentered the kitchen, a smile on her face. Simeon followed, looking somewhat more worried than his wife.

"We have news for you, dear," Rachel said.

Eliza's heart stopped. Rachel was smiling, but Simeon was scowling thunderously. Not good news, then.

Simeon put a hand on Rachel's arm and shook his head. "We shouldn't tell her now. We don't want to breed false hope."

"Nonsense, Father, some hope is better than no hope," the woman responded calmly.

"You'll make the poor girl worry, and she has worries enough."

"If I were her, I'd want to know," Rachel said, somewhat more sharply. "And the Bible says do unto others as you would have them do unto you. So if you won't tell her, I will."

Simeon laughed and stood back, taking his place against the wall near the hanging pots. "Well, it seems I have no choice."

Eliza, who had been watching this exchange with increasing fear, broke in at this point. "What are you two talkin' about?" she asked.

Rachel came to sit next to her, laying a gentle hand on her arm while her husband spoke. "Eliza, did you say that your last name is Harris?" Simeon asked kindly.

Eliza noticed a hitch in the question and bit her lip. Had it been a mistake to tell them that? "Yes, why? Have you seen a poster with my name on it?"

"No, but one of Van Trompe's sons just delivered a message. And I believe it concerns you."

Eliza waited, breathless at this news.

Simeon looked at her for a moment, then continued. "Van Trompe is delivering more friends from the Railroad later on today. And one of them goes by the name of George Harris."

Eliza burst out laughing, unable to contain the good news. "George?" she gasped, her heart overflowing with joy. "George is with Van Trompe? And coming here?"

Simeon's face broke into a smile at Eliza's reaction. "I thought he might belong to you! Yes, he's coming with two other runaways courtesy of Van Trompe. The man tells me that they arrived not long after he returned from bringing you here."

"Oh my!" she said, putting her hands to her cheeks. "Why would you ever want to keep such a thing from me?"

His face grew serious. "Because there are slave catchers involved. They went to the Van Trompe house looking for you, and Van Trompe fears that they'll attack his party on the road."

"Slave catchers?" she murmured. Haley, then, it had to be him. He'd tracked her here with some of his friends. And now George was in danger because of her. Her heart sank at the thought, and all the happiness she'd felt froze into a cold, hard ball in her stomach.

Simeon nodded, watching the emotions cross her face. "Child, the Lord has protected you so far, and you must pray that He continues to do so. Pray that He will protect your husband on the road here, and that He will protect us all in the coming days."

Eliza nodded, overwhelmed at the range of emotions in her heart. George, on his way here, to find her and Harry! But waiting for him on the road...Haley—with other slave catchers. What if he was caught and sent home to that terrible Harris to be punished? Killed in the process? But no, she told herself. George was the smartest man she'd ever met, and Van Trompe knew what he was doing. Surely they would make it there safely.

And when they arrived, they would go on to Canada. If they arrived at all. Because if they didn't arrive in time, she knew, she would have to go by herself. Haley was on the road to this very colony, and that meant he could show up at any time. She could no longer afford to stay here.

Suddenly Rachel's words came back to her. What if George didn't make it to Canada? What if she and Harry found themselves alone in that new country, unable to care for themselves, and without any friends or relations?

"Dear Lord, let him arrive safely, and soon," she whispered, turning her prayers to where they were most needed.

CHAPTER 31

The night was thickly dark around them, the air heavy with mist, and George wondered suddenly whether this would help or hurt them. They were loading their things—scant as they were—into Van Trompe's cart, making ready to set out. Van Trompe was strapping his best horses into the harness, having put the horse they came with into his own stable to recover, while George and Jim scooped forkfuls of hay into the back of the cart. Anita sat to the side, watching with an intensity about her eyes that George felt he could match.

They'd decided that they would leave in the middle of the night, when it was darkest, in the hopes of getting up the road before the slave catchers were able to organize themselves. Van Trompe had suggested a cart full of hay so that George, Jim, and Anita could hide in the roughage if necessary. Further, a cart of hay looked like nothing so much as a farmer going to market. Certainly no one would assume that they were transporting anyone.

George only hoped that he was right.

"And it'll give me a reason to be traveling north," the man noted, his fingers fumbling with the buckles on the harness. "Should anyone stop us, I'll have a ready answer for being on the road."

George nodded, seeing the wisdom of this statement. The hay would serve two very important functions then. Though he prayed that they wouldn't need either one.

"George, I need you over here," Jim said suddenly, arresting George's attention.

He walked toward the larger man, raising his eyebrows in question. "What is it?"

Jim hefted a shotgun—one of those from Van Trompe's wall, George thought—and held it out to him. "Need to teach you how to use one of these," Jim said roughly. "No tellin' who we'll meet on the road, and we'll need as many guns as we can get in a fight."

George shook his head. "I don't want anythin' to do with that gun, Jim. Can't I use one of the smaller pistols?" He couldn't have said why, but for some reason the smaller guns seemed less dangerous. Somehow friendlier.

Jim shook his head. "Those require more experience. Have to learn to aim them, practice at shootin' them, learn how to protect yourself. Shotgun is much easier to use."

George frowned. "Can't I just drive? Leave the shootin' to you and Van Trompe?"

Van Trompe appeared at his side at that point, also shaking his head. "That won't do, George. You don't know where we're going, and if someone passes us, they're bound to think it suspicious if they see a Negro driving a cart. Besides, what would you do if we met the slave catchers on the road?"

George nodded slowly, seeing what he meant, and turned back toward Jim. He hated the idea of handling the guns, which had only ever destroyed things in his experience, but given the situation, he understood why it might be necessary. This was, after all, just another step on his road back to Eliza and Harry.

Jim, seeing George's agreement, took the smaller man quickly through the steps of loading, aiming, and then shooting the gun. "Keep the butt against your shoulder, George, or the kick'll throw you down and break your nose for you," he muttered sharply, adjusting George's grip and stance once more. "And for God's sake, don't point it at anyone else. If you're not shootin', keep the gun pointed at the ground."

George nodded, trying to keep the details straight, and tried aiming one more time. It must have been good enough, for Jim huffed in satisfaction and turned away.

Van Trompe saw that the lesson was over and gestured to the three travelers. "Well then, if you two are finished, it's high time for us to be going. Sooner we're out there on the road, sooner we'll know whether we'll get to the next stop safely or not. Anita, George, into the back, if you please. Jim, if you'll ride with me, it would be a help. You're a free man now, so they can't do anything to you, even if they see you. But keep your traveling papers handy. You might need them."

George and Anita hustled into the back of the wagon, scooting under the hay and covering themselves as much as they could. At the front of the wagon, George could hear Jim and Van Trompe climbing up onto the bench. His heart raced with the idea that they were on their way. In the darkness ahead, they might find either safety or a party ready to attack them. Then the cart jerked and they were on their way.

They'd been driving for what felt like hours when George saw movement on the road behind them. He'd hollowed out a place in the hay so that he could see back the way they'd come and had been passing his time thinking about Eliza and Harry, wondering when he'd seen them again. He'd nearly fallen asleep, but then a glint of light broke out on the road behind them.

He snapped his mouth shut, staring intently into the dark, and waited. There. He saw it again—he was sure of it.

"Jim!" he hissed. "I think there's someone back there on the road behind us!"

Before Jim could answer, George realized that he was quite right: There were, in fact, three men on the road behind them. They were on horseback, and they were riding hard for the cart. He could see them clearly now, thanks to the lantern they had with them.

"That's them," he muttered, shifting nervously. One big man, one small, and one middle-sized. Who else could it be?

And how had they found them so quickly?

They were riding faster now, evidently having caught sight of the cart, and George's heart was pounding. Those men were going to catch them—he could already see it. No matter how hard Van Trompe's horses ran, they had a wagon behind them and the weight of several people. The slave catchers were going to pull abreast of the wagon, and soon.

"Stop! We need to inspect your wagon!" the largest man called out, his voice hoarse in the cold night. George bit his lip. That was Loker. He'd bet his life on it.

"Gentlemen, I think we've been found," Van Trompe muttered.

"Can't you go any faster?" Jim asked.

Van Trompe leaned forward over the reins and called to the horses, urging them to run faster, and after a moment the cart began to pull away from its pursuers. George grabbed at the side of the wagon, trying to steady himself against the bumping and jouncing of the cart, and Anita moaned beside him. But when he poked his finger through the hay and looked at the road behind him, he could see the slave catchers falling behind.

For a moment, he thought they might get away.

Then the slave catchers put their heels to their horses' sides and rode harder toward the wagon. Loker—George could recognize him from his size—pulled a gun from his belt and began shooting. The shots went wide, hitting the trees around them, but his intention was clear: he didn't mean to let Van Trompe and his cargo get away.

"He's firing at us," Van Trompe muttered. "Time for you two to get involved, Jim. Get them off us or they're going to catch us."

George fumbled with the gun at his side, knowing exactly what Van Trompe meant, but before he could pull it up, the man he recognized as Haley was at their side, reaching out for Van Trompe. The driver knocked Haley's hand away, shouting at him, but Haley was insistent. He was about to grab at Van Trompe again when Jim stood from his seat, steadied himself, and pulled out his two pistols. Haley, seeing the guns, pulled up suddenly, and when Jim fired he missed.

At the sound of the shots, another slave catcher—Marks, George suspected—screamed and slowed, shouting that he wasn't going to put his own life in danger for this chase.

"Your gun, Haley!" Loker shouted. "You waitin' to be shot before you start shootin'?"

"The boy might be in there!" Haley answered, obviously unwilling to take the chance. George heard him and caught his breath. This was the man after his son, he remembered. And he thought Harry might be in here and harmed in the gunfight. Rather than reassuring him, though, the thought made him furious.

He shot to his feet and pulled the shotgun up, barely taking the time to think before he let off a shot. Jim pushed him to the floor of the wagon a moment later, and none too soon, as several bullets rained down around them from behind. Van Trompe ducked over the reins, trying to avoid the bullets, and pushed the horses on. Jim sat up again and pointed his two pistols toward the pursuers, letting off two more shots.

George, thinking that this was his chance to eliminate the danger, tried to shoot again, but his gun misfired terribly. Beyond them, he heard Loker laugh.

"Can't even shoot right, can you boy?" he snarled.

"Try again, George," Jim said quickly. "Remember, load the gun, cock the hammer, and then pull the trigger!"

George followed Jim's instructions, struggling to focus amidst all the noise and movement. This had all been much simpler on the firm ground of Van Trompe's courtyard. When the gun was loaded and cocked, he pulled it up in front of him, settled the end against his shoulder, aimed, and pulled the trigger. This time the bullet hit Loker's horse, and the animal went down under him. As the large man and his horse went down, they crashed into Haley, knocking him from his own saddle. At first, George was shocked. Then he just smiled. He hated to shoot the horse, who hadn't done anything wrong, but now, when it was a choice between the horse's life and his own, he didn't feel that there was any other way.

As expected, Marks halted his pursuit, pulling his horse to a harsh stop. He, Loker, and Haley raged after the escaping cart, but with two men on the ground and one horse dead, their chase was effectively over. For the moment.

Van Trompe looked back, laughed once, and then turned forward again. "Good shooting, boys, good shooting," he congratulated them.

Jim clapped George on the back, agreeing, and George settled back into the cart, quite proud of himself. That was one step closer to Eliza and Harry then. And one step closer to freedom.

CHAPTER 32

Eliza sat in Rachel's rocking chair, gently rocking back and forth to put Harry to sleep. The boy had been fussy all day, and Eliza had been at her wits' end trying to both take care of him and keep her eye on the front door. The fact that Simeon had seen George was on her mind, and though she'd been overjoyed to hear of his presence, her joy had quickly turned to fear. The slave catchers were after him, Simeon had said, and Van Trompe had been worried. The farther into the day they got—without the Van Trompe party arriving—the more she'd worried that they'd been captured.

Harry had picked up on her fear, as children do, and spent the entire day worrying alongside her, though she'd never told him what was going on.

"Where's Papa, Ma?" he'd asked repeatedly. "Why isn't he here with us?"

Eliza had sighed, wondering how to answer. The child had noticed their flight from house to house and the changing environment—how could he not?—but had been truly heroic in his bravery. He hadn't questioned her often, partially because she'd acted like they were playing some sort of game, and now that he was asking, she wasn't sure what to tell him.

Now, exhausted with worrying over her child and husband all day, Eliza's own eyes drooped and closed. A part of her welcomed the rest and break from worrying, but the larger part of her mind woke her back up, reminding her that she was waiting for her husband and that he could be here at any moment.

She smiled at the thought, for she'd readied herself as best she could. She'd had a thorough bath and even ironed the dress she'd received from Mrs. Bird. Now, with her face and hair scrubbed fresh, she felt better than she had in days and hoped she looked it.

Harry snorted in her lap, drawing her attention, and she glanced down at him. The little man had been bathed as well, in preparation of his father possibly arriving, but Eliza didn't have the heart to keep him awake any longer. In fact, he was already asleep, his face relaxing into the gentle lines of a dozing child. She watched him for a moment and smiled. Then Eliza gently laid Harry down on a nearby sofa and wondered if she might have time for a short nap herself.

Then she shook herself. Of course she didn't. If God was watching over her family—as she thought He must be—George would arrive tonight. Tonight! And she didn't want to be caught sleeping.

Of course, in the end she did fall asleep, despite herself, and began to dream. She dreamt of a beautiful country—a land of green shores, pleasant islands, and bright, glittering water. A land where she and her family were free to do as they wanted without fear. A land where Harry got up every morning, played on the seashore, and never knew the feel of chains or whips.

In her dream she was alone, watching Harry play, though she somehow knew that George was nearby. Then, gradually, she began to hear his steps coming toward her. Before long she felt his arms around her, and his tears falling on her face.

She didn't want to leave the dream, having finally found George, but the wetness of the tears forced her awake. Her eyes fluttered open, then ran around the room as her brain struggled to remember where she was. She paused, then turned her eyes back to what she'd just seen, hardly daring to hope. She gasped at the sight that met her gaze.

"George!" she whispered, hardly daring to believe the vision. For there he stood in front of her, his face alight with a joyous smile, his cheeks wet with the tears he'd been crying.

Without another word, she jumped up and into his arms, holding him as tightly as she'd ever held anyone, and sobbing. "Oh George! I was dreaming of you, thinking that we were together as a family, and yet here you are! You're really here? I can hardly believe it!"

"Oh Eliza, my Eliza, I've missed you so," he whispered into her hair, his voice rough with his tears.

Eliza leaned back and looked at him, her blood rushing through her body with joy. He wasn't as neat and clean as he'd been when he was working at the factory, though he looked fit enough. And the rugged outfit he wore suited him, she thought—sharp black trousers and a shirt that must have been white at some point. A coat, not his own. There was also an air about him that she hadn't seen before —he was even more confident. More regal, somehow.

"Not as much as I've missed you," she answered solemnly. "I'm so glad to see you, George!"

Harry awoke at that point, from all the noise, and jumped suddenly to his feet. "Papa!" he shouted, his voice full of childish wonder. "You finally came!" He launched his small body from the chair into the air in front of George, who caught him quite cleanly and laughed aloud.

He reached out to pull Eliza against him as well, holding the family as he hadn't done in what seemed like forever. "I can't believe you left without me!" he laughed. "How did you manage it, Eliza? Where did you find the will to do such a thing? I never thought you'd leave the Shelby house, not without me goadin' you!"

"I didn't want to, but I didn't have a choice. You've heard? Uncle Tom told you?"

"Yes," George answered, squeezing her more tightly. "And you were brave to do what you did. I couldn't ask for any more."

Eliza laughed—a short, mirthless laugh that acknowledged the hopelessness of the situation. "I only did what you would have, George. And I'm sure you would have done it better."

"Me? I don't believe that. I'd never have dared to jump across the Ohio River."

"We did, Papa, we did!" Harry shouted, squirming joyously.

"Mamma jumped right onto that ice, and I told her where to go next! And we got across, and there was a man—"

Eliza looked up, surprised. "How did you…?"

"Andy and Sam," George answered quickly. "I ran into them in the forest outside Maysville, shortly after you escaped."

Eliza smiled, proud of herself despite her words. "Well, you obviously know about my trip. But how did you get out of Kentucky? How did you get here?"

George turned and pointed toward the doorway, and Eliza looked to see a large Negro man and an older woman. They stood in the doorway smiling at the reunion, though she was certain that she'd never seen them before.

"Eliza, these are my new friends, Jim and Anita. They helped me escape. I wouldn't be here if it weren't for them."

She smiled and walked toward them. Jim was a very large man, she noticed immediately. George was relatively tall at six feet, but Jim towered over him and was broader in both the chest and shoulders. He was dark-skinned and quite handsome, but no match for her keen, intelligent-faced George.

The woman next to him was older and rounder, but she had kind eyes and a face that was accustomed to smiling. Eliza liked her immediately.

"Thank you both for savin' my husband and bringin' him to me," she said warmly, striding forward to take the hands of these new friends. "I don't know what I would have done without him. You two have saved my life, and that of my son."

"Well, now, George did his own part," Jim answered, his voice pitched low. Eliza thought he looked slightly embarrassed at the praise, but she reached out to grasp his hand anyhow. "We mightn't have made it without him either."

Eliza stopped at that, remembering the man who had been pursuing them. "Haley and the slave catchers. Did you meet them on the road? How did you get past them?"

George frowned and gave Eliza a quick accounting of how they'd been driving and been accosted by Haley, Loker, and the reluctant Marks. "In the end, there was a gunfight, and two of their horses went down," he ended quickly, with a sharp glance at Jim. "They couldn't pursue us after that. We arrived safely some time ago."

"Oh George," Eliza breathed, awed despite herself. She'd always known that George was brave, but to think of him in a gunfight—having to defend himself—was almost more than she could imagine. "To think that you've learned to shoot a gun! And were in a gunfight just to get here!"

"It'll take more than guns to stop me, Eliza," he answered,

slipping an arm around her back and squeezing gently. "We have a ways to go, and I mean to see this through."

At that moment, Rachel entered and looked around the room. "Well, I see the family is back together at last. You must be hungry. Let me get breakfast started."

She walked to the sink where she began scrubbing potatoes. Before long, her daughter Mary appeared as well, bringing with her a side of bacon. Eliza was just about to move toward the sink to help with the preparations when Simeon appeared in the doorway, looking quite worried. He had a man with him, also dressed as a Quaker, but noticeably less clean and well kept than the other Quakers Eliza had met in her time here.

"Good morning, friends, I'm glad to see everyone here," Simeon began. Rachel turned to him, took in his frown, and frowned herself.

"Father, why do you look so worried?" she asked her husband.

"Friend Phineas has come with some news for our visitors here."

At that, the man named Phineas turned toward the group. "In short, the slave catchers that have been chasing you know of our village. They've learned that you're here—

though I don't know how, and may just be guessing—and are making plans to capture the lot of you."

The room went silent at the news.

Eliza was the first to come back to life. She turned to George, her heart racing and her body trembling, and took his hand. "Well then, we must go now. But where? And how?"

CHAPTER 33

George held Eliza tightly, his mind rushing from possibility to possibility. What were they to do? Where were they to go? He had no idea where they were, or how they should get to Canada. They had no money, no horses of their own. They were dependent on these Quakers, and though they seemed like kind enough folk, he disliked that immensely.

He disliked even more that Eliza was so frightened. She'd already been through so much on her own, and he hated to think of her going through anything else. They had to get her out of here, in any way possible, before those slave catchers arrived. Though his natural instinct was to fight his own battles, he would depend on these people—and gladly—if they could get his wife and son to safety.

CARL WATERS & DR. KAL CHINYERE

"Who are you?" he asked, directing his question to the stranger. "What are you talkin' about?"

"This is Friend Phineas Fletcher," Simeon answered. "He's seen and heard things that concern your party. Tell them, Phineas."

Phineas nodded. "Last night, on the way here, I stopped in a lone tavern about ten miles back on the road. I was tired from driving during the day, so I laid down on a pile of rugs in the corner, pulled a buffalo skin over me, shut my eyes, and went to sleep. But before dawn, I was awoken by the activity of three men that came rather noisily into the place and sat at a table near me. They were making such a ruckus and seemed almost intent on being overheard. In the end, I couldn't help but do just that—though I'll admit to some selfish curiosity on my own part. I didn't trust them from the moment I laid eyes on them and thought immediately that they might be up to no good."

"What did they look like?" George asked fearfully.

"One was large as a bear and loud, the other small, resembling nothing so much as a mouse."

"Loker and Marks," George confirmed. It could only be them. How was it that those men continued to find him, no matter where he went? Were they driven forward by the devil himself?

Phineas nodded. "You know them, then. They had another man with them—though I didn't see him clearly—and were talking about hiring two or three other men to help them catch some runaways. The smaller man said that he would arrange for two constables to join them as well, in order to make the whole thing legal. The third man was nondescript, for the most part, though he seemed sorely concerned with the wellbeing of a boy. Kept saying that he must get him back unharmed."

"Haley, it must be," Eliza muttered to George, squeezing his hand.

Phineas watched the couple and then nodded. "I see that you two know of these people. The small man seemed certain that you would be staying here, in our village, and that they could find you if they searched. He must know of our colony, and our work, though I daresay he's never had reason to visit here before. The larger man thought it better to come on you as you left, take you by surprise, so that they wouldn't have to deal with us. In the end, he won out. They've arranged to have seven or eight men in their party, and to take you on the road."

George gave Harry to Eliza and began to pace. Moving helped him to think, and it was important that he think quickly now. "If they know we're here, then we must leave now."

"No," Simeon answered quickly. "You're safe here, for the moment. They wouldn't come here during the day when we could see them approaching. They won't come until night. And even then, they'll have a time getting into and maneuvering through the colony itself."

George reached a wall and turned, pacing back the other way. "Then we'll stay here for the day and leave at nightfall."

"But they'll be waitin' for us on the road," Eliza said, her voice shaking. "Surely it's not safe to travel at all."

Jim pulled his pistols from his belt and eyed them. "We've handled them before. We'll do so again."

"But eight men, Jim, we'll be outgunned," Anita said sharply.

"Any man can carry a gun. Not all men are willin' to use it," Jim retorted.

"Friend Jim, I like your thinking," Phineas said, laughing.

"Friend Phineas, it's clear you were not born a Quaker. The old nature is still strong in you," Simeon chided. He turned toward the others, explaining. "Phineas became a Quaker for his wife and reverts to worldly thinking more often than we would like. It's one of the reasons we use him to transport people like you. He can relate to outsiders more than the rest of us can."

"And what would you have them do, Friend Simeon?" Phineas asked abruptly. "Sit and wait for their fates and do nothing about it?"

"Perhaps I can reason with these men. They must have families of their own."

"Yes," Jim agreed, grinning. "And while you're talking to them, I'll shoot them!"

Phineas laughed, though Simeon looked more worried at this statement. George, for his part, continued to pace. There must be a way out of this, he thought. He just needed to find it. Something that would get them away to safety, and with minimal loss of life. If he could avoid putting Eliza and Harry in danger, he would. And he'd do anything to keep them away from those guns. Suddenly he thought he had a plan. He stopped and turned to Simeon.

"How well do you know the northbound road out of the village?"

"Well enough, but not as well as Friend Phineas."

George turned to Phineas, his mind spinning with ideas. "And you? How well do you know it?"

"Quite well. I was a backwoodsman before I met my wife, and a hunter. I spent many months alone in the wilderness and know my way around."

George nodded. That was what he needed. "Do you know an area along the road where we can force our pursuers to walk or ride in single file? So that they expose themselves?"

Phineas began to rub his chin, thinking. He sat down for a moment, then stood and walked around a bit. Finally he said, "Yes, I know a place like that."

"Then I have a plan that should please all parties," George said, relieved. "We find this place that you speak of and make our way up along the path. If it's as narrow as I hope, we'll have to go single file. And then we'll hide at the top. Our pursuers—if they see where we go at all—will have to come single file as well. That way—" he aimed his fingers, using them as makeshift guns, and mimed shooting them, "we can pick them off if they come for us. They'll see that as well as we can, and with luck, they'll refuse to come up. Perhaps it'll get us free of them."

Everyone nodded in agreement, declaring that this was a wise move, and Eliza moved toward George.

"That's why I married you," she said, and kissed him soundly on the mouth.

George smiled, pleased. "And here I thought it was for my riches," he answered.

Everyone laughed, and Rachel called them to their breakfast. George followed the others to the table, ravenous, but paused when everyone else had sat down. He believed in his plan, truly, and thought it was the best way out of their predicament—their best chance at freedom—but he also worried that it wouldn't work, or that something would go wrong along the way. What if the slave catchers found them before they reached the designated place in the road? What if they caught his party unprepared?

If that happened, he told himself firmly, he would fight to the end, for he'd rather die fighting for his family than allow any of them to be taken back into slavery. With that final thought, he moved forward to the table, ready to embark on this one day with the Quakers.

CHAPTER 34

Eliza sat on the little bed, watching as George walked around the room, mumbling to himself. They'd slept some, but not much, and were now busy planning and preparing for the coming journey. Eliza held Harry close to her, her mind racing ahead of them to the road and the dangers they might find there. It was growing dark outside, and she didn't think it would be long before they were on their way, setting back out into the dangers of the world.

Still, her George was with her again, and he'd take care of them. She was sure of it.

"Your plan is ingenious, George," she said, partially to herself. "With luck, we'll get all the way to Canada without anyone bein' hurt. Thank God for that brain of yours."

"Thank God?" George scoffed. "If God were on our side, Eliza, we wouldn't need a plan at all. In fact, we wouldn't be in this situation. We would never have been born into a life where other men ruled over us, as if we were little better than animals. Lower than animals even, for at least the white men value their horses and dogs. We wouldn't have to worry about evil men tryin' to purchase our son, or chasin' us when we dared to seek freedom for him. We wouldn't have to worry about bein' arrested for seekin' our own freedom. It would never enter our minds, for we would be free men and women already, if God was truly on our side."

Eliza stood and went to him, laying a gentle hand on his arm. She'd heard these very arguments before but had never believed in them. She didn't believe that their situation was right—not a bit of it—but she did believe that God loved them, regardless of what the world did to them. Now, she thought, it was time for George to truly start to believe. For if God hadn't led them there, then who had? "Dear George, our time here is short, compared to our time in Heaven. And the Lord never promised us an easy life here. The selfish and hateful may prosper in this world—He says so himself. But He's told us that He'll never give us any more than we can stand. And the meek will prosper in the next life. He'll reward us when we get to Heaven. I'm sure of it. Until then, we must have faith."

George snorted. "So I must wait until I die for your Lord to reward me? That doesn't seem like a very fair deal."

"And hasn't He helped you on your journey here?" she asked gently, already knowing the answer. "Didn't He lead you to the tavern so that you would know I was safe? Didn't He then guide you to Jim and Anita, and from there to Van Trompe's house, so that you might come this far?"

"I admit that I've experienced some good fortune on my journey, yes," George answered, smiling despite himself.

Eliza smiled back, happy with this small victory. "And don't you think that means somethin'? Stop lookin' for the bad in the world, George, and start lookin' for the good. Instead of lookin' at what we don't have, look at what we do have, and give thanks for that."

"Give thanks for my empty pockets?" he asked sadly.

"The Lord has blessed you with the quickest mind I've ever met, George, and I have faith that your smarts will get us safely to Canada. That same intelligence will help you find work when we're there, to provide for our family. He blessed me with a kind mistress, who taught me how to sew, and that will help us too. He's blessed us with each other, hasn't he? And our son? Aren't those good things, for which we should be thankful?"

George took her into his arms and squeezed her tightly. "Yes," he whispered. "Yes, we have much to be thankful for.

And I'll try to think of it more, Eliza, I swear. Once we're safely away, and livin' in Canada, I'll try."

Just then, a knock came at the door. "Friends, it's time for you to leave," Simeon called through the wood.

George let go of Eliza, gave her one last look, and then turned and scooped Harry up in his arms. "Right," he said firmly. "Well then, little man, we're off on another adventure. Are you ready?"

Harry nodded gamely, and Eliza smiled. One step closer to Canada, and after this ride they might well be free. The thought of her son playing without fear made her heart soar, and she followed George out of the room feeling giddy and hopeful.

They met the others in the kitchen where Rachel had prepared food. She handed a full carpetbag to Eliza.

"Eliza, these are for you and yours. Children are always cold or hungry, so I've made sure to pack extra for your little one. And there are blankets in the wagon for you, and buffalo rugs for you to sit on."

"Oh Rachel," Eliza protested. "You've done so much for us already. I can't accept it."

"Nonsense," Rachel answered. "You'll take the provisions, and you'll remember me on your journey and know that I'm praying for your safety. You would do the same for us—I'm certain of it. Now go, go!"

Rachel shooed the couple out of the kitchen and into the small courtyard, along with Jim and Anita, and the small group found themselves facing a large covered wagon, already hitched to a team of two tall, strong horses. Phineas jumped down from the driver's bench and put a hand out to Eliza, ready to help her into the back of the wagon.

But George put out a hand, stopping him. "We don't need anyone's help beyond what we've already had," he said firmly. "I won't put anyone else's life at risk."

Eliza gaped at him, shocked. How could he refuse help now, when they were so close to escape?

Phineas laughed, seemingly of the same opinion. "Well you'll need a driver, George, so I'm not convinced that you can refuse help."

"Just lend me your wagon and give me directions, please. Jim and I have weapons. I'll drive and protect the front. Jim can protect the rear."

"Well, you're quite welcome to do all the shooting you want," Phineas answered patiently. "But I know a thing or two about the road, and I wouldn't feel right sending you out alone. Don't be too proud to accept help. You'll only put yourself and your family at risk."

Eliza looked from the Quaker to her husband, praying that George would let go of his stubborn insistence to do things for himself and let the man help them. Though she trusted George, she also knew that a smart person accepted help when it was offered.

Unfortunately, George wasn't ready to give in. "I won't involve you, Phineas. It's too dangerous."

Eliza laid her hand on his arm. "George, please," she murmured. "We can't do this on our own, and well you know it. We must have help if we're to make it safely. For me, George, and your son. Please."

George gave her a long, searching look and finally nodded. "For my wife and son then, Phineas," he acceded. "But Jim and I'll do the shootin'. You're just to drive."

Phineas nodded at this compromise and turned to Jim. "We must be off. I've engaged my friend Michael Cross to watch the road behind us. If men come after us, he'll alert me to the danger."

Jim scowled. "How will he watch the road behind us and reach the wagon to alert us at the same time?"

"Michael's horse is the fastest in Ohio. He'll reach us long before any pursuers do." Phineas laughed, looking well pleased with himself. "But are your pistols in order? If those men do reach us, you'll be forced to defend yourselves." He glanced from Jim to George and back again. Jim nodded, patting his pistols, and Phineas nodded in response.

"Then let's be off. Quickly, women and children—child— into the back of the wagon. You'll want the most protection, and that's the safest place for you."

Without further ado, George, Jim, and Phineas bundled Anita, Eliza, and Harry up into the back of the wagon, tossing blankets, hampers, and buffalo skins after them. Eliza settled Harry under one particularly heavy fur, then turned to the back of the wagon again. George and Jim both sat there, their legs hanging over the back of the wagon, their guns at the ready. Phineas had moved to the front of the wagon and assumed his position as driver. He called out a quick warning, then snapped the whip. With a jolt, the wagon began to move forward, taking them away from the Hallidays' home and out onto the road.

Eliza watched the house receding behind them and felt her eyes filling with tears. She'd made—and then said good-bye to—many new friends in the last few days and was beginning to feel the strain of it. She was certainly ready to make a home again, to settle into one place, meet people, and have a hearth to call her own.

In Canada, she realized. The next time she would be at home was Canada, when she and George made their own lives. If they arrived safely. Suddenly, and despite her earlier words about faith, she began to doubt. What if the Lord didn't plan for them to make it to Canada safely? What if His plan was for them to be taken captive, or—worse—for one of them to die? She huddled close to Harry and pulled him to her in silent protest at this thought.

Then, taking a deep breath, she turned back toward the rear of the wagon. Her husband was there—straight, tall, and proud—and it gave her some comfort. He would see them safe, she thought—he and their new friends. She glanced at the road behind them, wondering if she should watch as well and warn them of any danger. But no, she thought. George and Jim were watching, and they could be trusted with the responsibility. Besides, their past lay in that direction—the South, and all the things they'd run from. Things she hoped never to see again.

Ahead of them, though…that was Canada, and the future, and their life as a free family. That was the direction she wanted, and where she would look. She resolutely turned her eyes toward the front, to peek through the small opening there at the road ahead of them. The road to Canada. To freedom.

CHAPTER 35

The ride was uncomfortable, but George knew that the speed was necessary; they had to get to their chosen position in the road before anyone caught up to them if his plan was to work. Around them, the oaks and pines of the northern territories flew by, their branches whistling in the winter night's wind.

"Oak trees there—best wood for furniture makin'," Jim said, pointing out the thick, wide-spreading trees. "Hard wood, it is, and beautiful when it's polished up."

George nodded, but didn't answer. Jim was simply trying to pass the time, he knew. He just couldn't bring himself to respond. They'd been driving for only a short while, and already he was nervous. The slave catchers had known that the party would be leaving the Quaker village, and it didn't take a genius to guess which way they'd be going. Those trees seemed like nothing so much as places for the catchers to lie in waiting. Were they setting out a trap on the road ahead of them? Had they already left the tavern Phineas spoke of, to chase after George and his family?

Had Phineas and Simeon's fears caused them to leave too late, so that the slave catchers were already on top of them?

He turned back to the road behind them, straining his eyes to see through the gloom. Hearing a click next to him, he turned to see Jim doing the same, his pistols in hand and at the ready. George himself still had Van Trompe's shotgun with him, primed and ready to shoot if he saw any sign of danger.

Jim turned to George and grinned, his teeth a flash of white in the darkness. George did his best to smile back, but soon turned again to the road, nervous lest someone sneak up on them in the dark. So far, the journey hadn't been a pleasant one. The night was far too dark for them to enjoy much of the scenery, and the wagon wheels too loud to allow for much conversation. But they were making good time, he thought, and that was the important thing. Besides, the lack of distractions made it easier to focus on the road.

∼

They had been riding for a while, but George was still wide awake, his eyes beginning to feel sore from staring into the dark. He turned, thinking to pull a buffalo skin over him to protect him from the cold, and noticed that Jim was still awake as well, though looking significantly bored. At the front of the wagon bed, the women and Harry were all slouched together, obviously asleep. On the driver's bench, Phineas sat singing and whistling to himself, sounding very awake. George stifled a smile, then shot a look of annoyance at Jim. The man was meant to be watching out for the rest of them, after all, and instead looked as if he might fall asleep at any moment.

George had just opened his mouth to say so when he heard the sound of hoof beats on the road behind them. He whirled back toward the road, his heart racing. Who was that? The horse was flying along the road—he could hear that much from the hoofbeats. But there was only one horse. He peered through the blackness, praying that it was Phineas' friend and not one of the slave catchers, riding ahead alone.

"Must be Michael," Phineas called back quietly. "I'd know the sound of that horse's gallop anywhere."

George kept his eyes focused on the road. Even if Phineas was right and that was Michael behind them, there was only one reason for the man to be coming at that speed. The slave catchers were on their way.

Then he saw him: a slight man crouched over the neck of a large horse, who was indeed flying across the ground. George pulled his weapon up and Jim readied his pistols, neither of them willing to believe that this was indeed a friend. George spared a quick glance into the wagon. Both women had woken up at the noise. Eliza now held Harry firmly in her lap, her hand over his mouth, and her eyes as large as saucers.

"He's in Quaker garb," Jim noted suddenly, dropping his pistols. "He's a friend after all."

"But here to tell us that the slave catchers are after us," George added, wishing Jim would keep his pistols trained on the road behind them.

Phineas had noted the same and pulled back on the reins to slow the horses. Within moments, the man had caught them. George, still untrusting, stood up and pointed his shotgun at the man.

"Friend, that's very unnecessary," the man muttered and Phineas laughed.

"That's definitely Michael," he told his party, slowing even more.

At this, George dropped his shotgun. "What news?"

"They're about a half mile back but coming fast," Michael answered quickly. "Eight or ten of them, by my count. And they're hot with liquor, swearing and foaming like wolves. Been in some tavern or other, getting themselves all riled up."

Phineas grunted. "Well, we're almost to the spot where we plan to meet them. But we must hurry." With that, he slapped the reins across the horses' rumps and started them into the night again, making haste for the chosen position. Michael galloped along beside them, throwing his lot in with theirs. George and Jim watched the road, sweating at the danger.

It took them only minutes to reach the spot where they planned to make their stand. Phineas and Michael pulled their horses to a stop, and the party began to hurry out of the wagon. Behind them, George could hear the slave catchers, their galloping loud in the silence. They were indeed shouting and cursing, their horses racing along the road. They'd reach the spot in a matter of minutes, he thought.

"Hurry, Eliza," he muttered. "We must hurry." He handed her out of the wagon, then reached in to quickly transfer Harry to the ground.

On the other side of them, Phineas and Jim were helping Anita out of the cart and wrapping her warmly in a blanket.

"George, ready your weapon and come behind us," Phineas said quietly. "Michael, tie your horse to the wagon and drive ahead to Amariah's. Ask him to bring some friends to talk to those men. Perhaps they can make the slave catchers listen to good sense. The rest of you, follow me." So saying, he turned and strode into the woods, leaving Jim, Anita, Eliza, Harry, and then George to follow into the darkness.

George turned just before they entered the woods, taking one last look at the road. Michael was disappearing up ahead, racing for the house Phineas had spoken of. He turned and gazed in the other direction, scanning the darkness closely. On that side, Haley's party was just coming into view, their horses breathing heavily. They did indeed have ten men. He bit his lip; that was more than he and Jim could handle, he thought. More than they'd counted on, certainly.

Suddenly one of them called out, "They've escaped on foot into the woods! Quick, to the side of the road!"

George whirled and caught up with his own group. "Phineas, they know we're on foot!" he hissed. "How much farther is it?"

"Don't talk!" Phineas answered. "Run!"

George shut his mouth and darted after the others, dodging through the trees and hurdling bushes as he came to them. Behind him, he could hear the slave catchers crashing through the brush after them. They were making an ungodly amount of noise, but it covered the noise of George's party, and he hoped for a moment that they would become confused and miss him and his friends entirely. The woods around them were coming alive with small animals and birds—all darting into the sky or deeper into the forest to escape the men invading their territory. Perhaps the birds or animals will distract them as well, he thought breathlessly. Perhaps it would work after all.

Before Haley and his friends had a chance to catch up with them, they found themselves at their destination. Phineas motioned for them to follow, then dashed up a new pathway. George shot a glance upward and saw that the path led to a narrow passage, which traveled between two sharp, jutting mountains. The chasm wasn't long, but it was narrow and steep, and it forced them to ascend in single file. Phineas went first, carrying Harry, and Jim followed, helping his mother. Eliza and George brought up the rear.

At the top of the passage, they found shelter behind a tumble of boulders.

"Phineas, this is the perfect place," George muttered, turning back toward the trail behind him. "They'll have to approach in single file, just as we did, and Jim and I will be able to take care of them one at a time—if they're stupid enough to follow at all. No man in his right mind would walk that path, knowin' a man stood above him ready to shoot."

The party grew quiet then, the women drawing farther back behind the stones while Jim and George took up their positions at the head of the trail. George could hear Haley's party coming, but he wasn't afraid. Not anymore. This was exactly what he'd been hoping for: A chance to rid himself of those slave catchers once and for all, and to protect his family.

For the first time, he thought that God might actually be on his side.

CHAPTER 36

George checked Jim's position, then stepped into the passage itself to better see the men below. The cliffs rose sharply up on both sides of him, penning him in. For a moment he wondered if he was making himself an easy target, but the sky behind him was still black, he reminded himself; they wouldn't be able to see him unless he drew attention to himself.

"They'll be easy to pick off," he said quietly. "Fair game for our guns."

"Easy pickin's," Jim muttered in agreement.

George paused, then spotted the group of ten men below them, just coming up to the opening of the passage. They grouped themselves there, staring up the passage toward George's group. George wasn't sure how they'd found him,

275

but they didn't act as though they had any doubt about where he'd gone.

"You coons are fairly treed now, aren't ya?" one of the men shouted up, confirming George's suspicions.

"I saw them go up there myself," Loker answered, "and I mean to follow them. Don't have nowhere to hide up there. Won't take long to ferret them out."

"But they might fire on us from those rocks up there, Loker. We won't have any shelter," Marks answered. "It's madness to go up this path without some sort of cover."

George laughed at this. He didn't respect the little man, but Marks was certainly the only one in their group that had any intelligence to speak of.

Loker, however, didn't seem to appreciate the wisdom of the little man's statement. "Always out for savin' your skin, Marks. Never willin' to take a chance! But mark my words: those darkies're too scared to fire on us. Probably cowerin' behind those rocks, just prayin' that we don't come after 'em."

George narrowed his eyes at that. Too afraid to fire on them? Why, he'd show them exactly how afraid he was when the time came.

"And why shouldn't I save my skin?" Marks asked suddenly.

"I've only got the one. And those darkies do fight like devils sometimes. I'm not interested in dying for this here mission. That gal ain't worth that much to me."

Now, George thought it was time for him to add to their conversation. "Gentlemen, who are you down there, and what do you want with us?" he called out.

"We're looking for a group of runaways!" the man named Haley shouted back. "One of them is a woman who stole a boy that belongs to me."

It sent chills up George's spine to hear his son spoken of in that way, and his anger began to burn hotly in his stomach. These were the men who would try to take his son from him then. And his wife. His family. But he held his tongue, hoping that Marks would talk the rest of the party out of coming up the passage.

"One George Harris is who we're lookin' for!" Loker added. "Eliza Harris, and their son, all of them runaways."

George gritted his teeth. As long as he was willing to fight these men, he thought, he might as well be honest. "I'm George Harris!" he shouted. "My family and I are now free people. Please, leave us in peace. Let us go our own way. We don't wish any violence, but we won't hesitate to shoot if you force our hands!"

There was a long pause from the clearing below, and he watched the hunters closely. They were staring at each other as if they were surprised to hear a slave speak at all, much less speak with intelligence and logic.

This just made him hate them even more. They truly didn't believe that his people were human. Why, they didn't know what to do with themselves when a Negro spoke reasonably to them! And he doubted any of them would be able to understand a Negro who believed that he had the right to freedom.

"I have constables here would say otherwise, boy!" Marks finally called out. "Your freedom isn't guaranteed by law!"

"Those constables serve a law that was written by white men for white men," George answered gruffly. "That's not our law, and this isn't our country! As such, I say we do not have to abide by your laws! Rather we shall make our own! We just want to leave and make our own lives."

A gunshot rang out from below in answer, and George ducked down behind a boulder. So it was going to be that way, was it? Eliza screamed at the sound, and he growled. If they were going to start a gunfight, he'd be more than happy to finish it.

"Friend George, I think you should hide before you

continue this conversation," Phineas called out. "Get you to safety before you're shot."

George ignored him. "Jim, the first man who comes up gets a bullet between the eyes, do you understand? While you reload, I'll shoot the next, and so on."

"But George, you are no expert with a gun. What if you miss?" Eliza gasped. "What will become of us?"

Jim held up both his pistols. "I have two guns to add to George's, and it's mighty hard to miss a target if you have three guns pointed at it. Don't you worry, Miss Eliza. George and I'll keep you all safe."

At that, Loker's voice rang out from below again. "I'm goin' up after them! I never was afraid of darkies, and I ain't goin' to be now! Who's comin' with me?"

George peeked out from behind the boulder. Loker was indeed striding up the passage, springing from rock to rock in his hurry to capture their party. George watched him, rather surprised at this show of recklessness, then shook himself into action.

"Here he comes, Jim," he murmured. "Are you ready?"

Instead of answering, Jim shot. The first bullet went wide, but he pulled up his second pistol and sent another shot after Loker, hitting him in the left shoulder. Loker whirled away at the shot, clutching his shoulder, and howled in pain. He fell against the wall of the passage, sending down a shower of smaller rocks and soil, and George breathed out in relief. Then he stopped, shocked. To his horror, the man had turned back toward the passage and was still coming up after them. Quickly, as if his life depended on it.

"George, shoot him! I have to reload," Jim snapped, dropping to the ground with his pistols.

George stepped into the passage, his heart racing, and braced himself. This was the moment he'd been waiting for —the moment when he could take a real hand in saving his family. His first step toward ending the slave trade, by taking out one of the slave catchers personally. He pulled the shotgun up, breathed out, and pulled the trigger. But nothing happened. He pulled the trigger again, unable to believe this bad luck, but received nothing. The gun was jammed—and at the worst possible time.

George looked up to see Loker almost upon them. Instead of pausing, he charged the larger man, running as hard as he could into Loker's midsection. He didn't have much hope; the man was far larger than him and would surely shrug the attack off. To his surprise, though, the man fell sharply backward, seemingly hampered by the shot in his shoulder and the steep trail behind him.

Loker took one large step backwards, tripped on some loose gravel, and began to tumble, grabbing desperately for the walls of the chasm. The shale on the walls was too loose to support him, though, and he rolled faster and faster down the trail.

Unfortunately, George's momentum took him the same way. He stumbled forward, the chasm opening up in front of him, and would have followed Loker's progress but for Jim, who reached out and grabbed his shirt at the last moment.

"Where are you tryin' to go? You tryin' to leave me here to do all the work?" Jim asked, grinning wryly.

George recovered his feet and gave a nervous grin back, but he could feel his heart hammering away at his ribs. That had been too close.

"He can't have survived that," Phineas noted from above them. "No man could survive that fall."

George followed his friend's gesture toward the bottom of the mountain, thinking the same. Surely that would be the end of Loker. At the base of the trail, the large man was lying quite still in a crumpled heap in a nest of crushed grasses and small weeds. George watched closely, praying that the man wouldn't rise again. If their leader was down, perhaps the rest of the party would leave them in peace.

"Loker! Loker! You dead?" cried Marks, shaking the man roughly.

To George's horror, Loker opened his eyes and shook his head. "No darkie can kill me!" he yelled. "Help me up! They're goin' to get away!"

Before they could move to help him, though, Jim shot in their direction. Everyone below froze. "That was a warnin' shot!" he shouted. "The next man who moves dies! My friend has asked you to leave us alone, and I'll say it again. We want to go our own way, and we'd sure appreciate it if you just leave us to it."

"Don't listen to him!" Loker yelled. "Help me up!"

Marks, however, had already started back through the woods. "We need reinforcements, Loker! These men mean to kill us, and you're hurt. We must go for help!"

"What?" Loker sputtered, infuriated. "Leave me?"

But no one answered him. Although some of the men had tried to get Loker on his feet, they'd soon given it up. The man was too big, George thought, and far too injured for them to get him off the ground. Marks was right, he realized; they needed a doctor for their friend, and some sort of protection from George and Jim's guns.

Their best bet was, in fact, to leave Loker for the time being, and come back with reinforcements. The rest of the party was shuffling slowly after the smaller man now, looking regretfully back at the man they were leaving behind. George felt as though he could have risen up and cheered. Leaving, they were leaving!

After a few minutes, the base of the trail was clear but for Loker's broken body. George stared down, surprised. "I think they really did leave him," he whispered.

"Could be a trap," Jim answered, equally surprised. "Can't imagine anyone leavin' their friend like that."

"It's no trap. They're cowards," George said. "They'd rather leave him than put themselves in danger." He walked over and grabbed one of Jim's pistols, then made his way slowly down the trail. As he walked, he kept a keen eye on the forest, watching out for any sign of the slave catchers. But no one appeared, and when he reached Loker, the man was still very alone.

"They're gone!" George shouted up to his friends.

Loker opened his eyes and looked up at George. "So you mean to kill me, boy? While I'm layin' here broken, rather than in a fair fight? Guess I couldn't expect anythin' better from a darkie like you. Go on then, shoot me. Don't think you've got the guts to kill a man at close range."

George didn't answer. He just lifted the pistol, aimed it, and put his finger on the trigger.

CHAPTER 37

By the time Eliza caught her breath and moved to look out on the trail again, the gunfight was over. She breathed a prayer of thanks to her Lord for that much, at least, and then started counting heads. Anita and Phineas were with her, behind the rocks, and seemingly quite safe. Harry, of course, was tucked against her chest, though she'd had to hold him tightly to keep him from running out and helping his father, brave lad that he was.

Glancing out at the trail head, she could see only Jim, though, standing tall and unhurt. He was watching the pathway closely, as if watching something very interesting, and her gaze sharpened. Where was George? What had happened? Then Jim called something down to the trail below, and she realized that George had gone down toward the forest below.

She gasped. What was he doing? Going after those men, rather than turning with the rest of the party and running for safety? Nervous, she handed Harry to Anita and stepped out from behind the stones. When nothing happened, she darted forward to stand next to Jim and gaze down the trail at the forest below. What she saw shocked her to her fingertips.

The man Loker was lying helplessly on the ground, obviously very badly hurt and unable to stand. George stood over of him, speaking lowly and holding the pistol to Loker's forehead, his finger on the trigger.

"George, no!" she screamed, rushing down the trail without thinking. Loker had done more to her than any of them, but she couldn't allow George to kill him. She couldn't bear the thought of George bloodying his hands in that manner.

George glanced up, confused, and dropped the gun to his side.

"George, please don't kill him!" Eliza huffed, making her way down the chasm.

Loker laughed from the ground, sneering up at George. "And now your wench is tellin' you what to do! Boy, you've gone from one master to the next."

George moved forward and put one foot firmly on Loker's

shoulder. "Eliza's my wife, boy, and I'll thank you to speak of her with respect." He pressed down slowly, putting all his weight on the man's injured shoulder, and Loker groaned loudly in pain.

Eliza grimaced at the sound, and she could see George doing the same, though he leaned over the white man and snarled, "Mind your tongue!" Standing, he looked back up at her. "This man deserves to die, Eliza. It's no more than he would have done to us."

She'd finally reached his side and put a gentle hand on his arm. "That's not for you to decide, George, and well you know it. Besides, in his condition, he can't keep us from goin' north. He can't harm us anymore, George. Killin' him would just be spiteful."

George shook his head, always stubborn. "If I don't kill him, he'll do this to another family, Eliza, and then another."

"You don't know that."

Loker laughed at that—a loud, snarling laugh. "Oh girl, I can promise you I'll be doin' just that. Darkies like you, 'scapin' from your rightful owners, just askin' to be caught? It's easy money."

George stomped down on Loker's shoulder again, and the

man yelped. Eliza just looked calmly down at him though, knowing in her heart that what he said was true.

"George, I know how you feel. I should hate this man as well, maybe more than you. He would have taken my child from me, killed my husband. He would have sold me down the river, never to see my family again. He is a despicable man who profits from the sufferin' of others." She glanced up at her husband, her anger building as she spoke. Yes, she understood why George hated this man, and she couldn't blame him for his actions.

That didn't mean she agreed with them.

"Then I shall end his life, for your sake as well as mine," George muttered, lifting the gun again.

Eliza put a hand out to stay his action and shook her head. "Killin' him will make you no better than he is."

"Maybe I'm not any better than he is." This response was both bitter and hopeless, and Eliza's heart broke a little. She took George into her arms, holding him tightly, and stroked his back.

"I don't believe that, George," she whispered. "If that were true, I'd never have married you, and Harry wouldn't love you as much as he does."

George drew away and looked up at the head of the trail where Anita stood, holding Harry and watching them.

"Is this what you want to teach our son, George? Or do you want to teach him to forgive and live a better life?"

George paused for a long moment, and Eliza held her breath. They didn't have much time for him to make this decision—those other slave catchers would be back soon, and they still had a long journey ahead of them.

Still, it was important that George decide this for himself.

Finally he spoke, calling out so that those above them could hear him. "Jim, Phineas, can you come down here and help me get this gentleman on his feet? He's in need of assistance." He cast a shy smile at Eliza and then turned toward the man on the ground.

Moments later, Phineas was at the bottom of the chasm, looking at Loker's injuries. He ripped off Loker's shirt, wrapped it around the man's shoulder as a sling, then sat back.

"Well, the shoulder doesn't look good and you've lost quite a bit of blood, friend. This bandage might support the shoulder, though, and I've tried to stop the bleeding. I expect you'll make it until we can find you some shelter."

Loker scowled, despite this show of good will. "You fancy yourself a surgeon, Quaker?"

Phineas laughed. "No. But I've seen a good many injuries and had a few myself. Your injuries are bad, but none of your major bones are broken. I think you'll live."

George and Jim crouched down next to them, and the three friends worked together to lift Loker to his feet.

"Let's take this brute to the road," George said quietly. "Michael will be back with the wagon soon."

"And then we leave," Jim added. "The sun is already risin'. We must get to our next stop before someone else sees us."

The three men shuffled forward, half-supporting and half-carrying Loker, with the women following quietly. The sun was indeed rising behind the mountains now, and Eliza could see the first rays leaking up into the sky. It would be full light soon. It took them more time than they thought it would to get through the forest, and by the time they arrived, she was beside herself with worry. The sun was up now, and they were late on their journey. Still, she watched with pride as George hefted Loker up into the waiting wagon. He'd made the right decision, and she thought she was more proud of him now than she'd ever been.

"We'll take him to Amariah's, where Grandma Stephens can

doctor him," Michael told them, already climbing into the seat. "In the meantime, I suggest you folks get into the wagon as well. There are other slave catchers in the area, and they'll track you if they can."

Jim, Phineas, and George exchanged one glance, communicating a million worries between each other, and then the group hurried into the wagon themselves, crouching down to avoid notice on the journey to the next farmhouse.

CHAPTER 38

George waited as patiently as he could, biting his tongue against his need to travel more quickly. According to Phineas, they were getting close to the next stop. They were going to a house that belonged to the Quaker Amariah Stephens, where they would find food and some shelter until night fell again. While they drove, George and Jim had reclaimed their positions at the back of the wagon and now looked back toward the road, watching closely for anyone on their trail. George was glad to be able to watch out in this way and tried to enjoy the scenery as much as possible.

"What happens if someone sees us though?" he muttered, partially to himself. Although they were armed, he still worried that someone would see them and turn them in.

Beside him, Jim snorted. "Stop worryin', George. This isn't a slave state. It's common for Negroes to travel through here as free men."

George gripped the shotgun harder and took a deep breath. "I'll stop worryin' when I'm safely in Canada, and my family with me. Until then, I have bullets for anyone who tries to take my wife or my child from me."

Jim gestured to the bed of the wagon behind them. "Like him?"

George turned to look at Loker, who was riding in the wagon with Eliza, Harry, and Anita. His eyes were closed, but the pain was evident on his face. George would have thought he was dead if he hadn't seen his chest rising and falling. The man was getting what he deserved, and no mistake, but George had meant what he said when he told Eliza that he wouldn't kill him.

"He tried to take your family from you," Jim said gently. "Yet you let him live."

"We couldn't just leave him there," George snapped, turning back toward the road behind them.

Jim laughed, slow and soft. "Well that's debatable. But it's too late to do anythin' about it now. Just hope you don't come to regret it."

~

round midday, they arrived at the new Quaker village and were taken toward Amariah's farmhouse. The men helped Loker out of the wagon, leaving the women to their own devices, and supported him as he hopped into the small, simple house. There, Dorcas, Amariah's mother, was called to the kitchen to treat the slave catcher. George and Jim left Loker there to her ministrations and returned to the courtyard at the front of the house.

"We'll be taking the wagon back south now," Phineas told them with a sad expression on his face. "Can't be going any farther with you, but you're in good hands. Amariah will see you on the next stage of your journey, and with God's good will, you'll be in Canada soon."

George nodded, though he was sorry to see this new friend go. They watched Phineas climb into the wagon, give a wave to his fellow Quakers, and put the reins to his horses' rumps. A moment later, they were staring at nothing but the dust of the wagon, Phineas having taken his leave.

"Well, there goes another friend," Jim said quietly.

George didn't respond, but turned back to the house. He would miss Phineas and his quick wit, but there were other things to think of right now. Namely, getting his family on to the next step of the journey.

Inside, he found the family sitting down to a large lunch, put on by Amariah and his wife. Eliza and Harry were already sitting at the table, helping themselves to fried chicken, ham, potatoes, green beans, and a sauced dish that George didn't want to guess at. His mouth watered at the thought of food, and he realized suddenly that he hadn't eaten a full meal in some time.

When he sat down, though, his stomach soured and his appetite disappeared. Indeed, he wasn't sure that he could eat at all. There was still too much to be done.

"We need a plan," he said quietly. "What's the fastest, safest way to get from here to Canada?"

"Friend George, you've just arrived," Amariah said kindly. "Eat. Rest. We'll keep you safe. We can discuss a plan tomorrow."

George shook his head. "There are men out there who will be comin' after us. I don't think they'll stop, no matter what we do. I cannot rest while they're makin' their own plans. Jim, you've come this way before. How did you do it?"

"Went through Sandusky at night," Jim said around a mouthful of food. "Gave twenty dollars to a man named

Gene, who took my money and pointed me toward a Negro cabin on his ship. Next thing I know, I'm in Canada."

George sat back, his mind reeling. "Well, that doesn't seem too difficult."

"That's not the way it is anymore," Amariah cut in. "With the new Fugitive Slave Act, things have changed. Slave catchers are more aggressive. People are less likely to let you on their ships."

"This man doesn't allow Negroes on his ship anymore?"

"Gene is still taking tickets for his boats, but the slave catchers are on the wharf now, and they know what—and who—to look for. They prevent runaways from getting to Gene at all. They now question the right of any Negro going to Canada. Free or not."

"And this Gene, is he an abolitionist?"

Amariah laughed. "No. Simply underpaid by his employers and willing to make some extra money in whatever way he can. A man without real principles who will end up being your friend, thanks to his lack of strong beliefs one way or another."

George sat back, thinking. "So we need a way to get past the slave catchers, and to Gene."

Dorcas walked into the room at that point, interrupting the conversation, and turned to George. "Friend George, Friend Loker has asked to speak to you."

George frowned. "I don't have time for Loker at the moment, Ms. Dorcas. It's him and his kind that have put us in this situation. But thank you kindly."

Dorcas put a hand on his shoulder. "I believe you should reconsider, George. He can answer many of your questions."

Dorcas left the room, and George thought on her words as he paced. He then reluctantly walked toward the room where Dorcas was treating Loker. Behind him, Eliza, Jim, and Anita trailed along. Loker and Dorcas were in the middle of an argument when they arrived, the man lying in the one and only bed in the small room.

"I told you I needed somethin' for the pain!" Loker was snarling.

Dorcas gave him a long, patient look. "And I told you that I would give you something for the pain after you'd helped these people," she answered pointedly.

George hid a grin at that and stepped into the room. Loker looked up at him, his color somewhat better now than it had been.

"You all need to head into Sandusky as soon as possible," he said abruptly, obviously disliking the fact that he'd been forced. "The longer you wait, the more eyes you'll have lookin' for you."

"And why should we trust you?" George asked suspiciously.

"I won't get any medication for my pain until I help you," Loker muttered darkly, "but you brought me out of that forest when my own friends left me. Marks left me, and as far as I'm concerned he forfeited his part of the bounty when he did that. Don't want him or Haley collectin' nothin' with the way they've acted."

George drew back, surprised at this pettiness, but had to admit that it made a certain sort of sense. He would never have treated his own friends thusly, but then again he didn't expect that his friends would have left him on his own in the middle of a forest. "Tell me more."

"Dress so that they won't recognize you as runaways. We sent your descriptions to Sandusky, so you need to look like someone other than yourselves."

George nodded. "And Jim and his mother?"

"We weren't after the old woman or the big darkie. Had no idea who she was and didn't know who you were travelin' with. Thought he was a free black. They won't be lookin' for those two."

George was silent at that. Jim and Anita were free then. Only George's family was in danger. Although this made him glad for Jim and Anita, it also reinforced the lack of balance in the situation. He, Eliza, and Harry were in danger, merely because of their bad luck. Jim and Anita were safe because their luck had been better.

"Don't care if you hear my words or not," Loker added harshly. "I won't profit from your capture no more, and I won't have Haley or Marks makin' anything off it either. Not after what they did."

Suddenly George shot into action. "Right, we must leave this evenin' then, and we must have disguises. And if the disguises don't work, we'll have our pistols. Right, Jim?"

Jim heaved a great sigh and shook his head. "You heard the man, George. They aren't looking for us. Only for you. Don't think…don't think Ma and I will be goin' with you."

"What?" Anita and Eliza gasped in unison.

"Why not?" George asked, shocked.

"Didn't agree with you savin' that man, George, though I didn't say anything. But I won't follow you into an obvious trap, based on this man's word. He's misleadin' you, and it's easy to see as much. We have too much at stake to fall for that."

"Do you have a better way to get to Canada? A route that we could use instead?" At the thought, George's heart soared. He wanted to keep this group together, for Jim made him feel more comfortable, and if the large man had another way to make the journey...

"Not yet," Jim answered. "But I mean to stay here until I can come up with one."

"Jim, we can't wait," Eliza said quietly. "Those slave catchers will find us here."

"Yes, we have too much at risk to wait with you," George finished, his heart falling at the thought. They would be separating then, unless they could find a compromise.

Jim nodded once. "I understand. We'll be partin' ways then. But I have faith that we'll meet again in Montreal. The Lord has brought us into each other's lives for a reason, and I don't think this is the end of it."

George grasped Jim's shoulder warmly, then turned toward Eliza. "Eliza, we must decide on our disguises, and quickly. We leave within two hours."

Eliza grinned, despite the news that they'd be leaving Jim and Anita behind. "Don't worry, George, I know exactly how we'll dress. No one will ever recognize us."

He turned to leave the room but paused, another thought

occurring to him. When he turned back to Loker, he saw the other man staring after him, his anger now turned to someone else. George paused, then made his way back toward the bed.

He didn't have much use for Loker, overall, but there were one or two things still to discuss. If what he had in mind worked, Loker might be of some additional use to them.

CHAPTER 39

George was staring at his wife, trying not to laugh. He wasn't succeeding.

"Am I walkin' more like a man now?" she asked, turning to him again. "I'm tryin' to stomp more. Take longer steps. Look more confident. Is it workin'?"

"You're far too beautiful to be a man," George snorted out, trying to stifle his laughter.

"But my hair is gone!" Eliza said, putting a hand up to her head. "How can I be beautiful without my hair?" Her voice turned into a wail, and George stood and took her in his arms, running his hands through her newly shorn hair.

"There there. It was your idea to dress like a man," he murmured. "And it'll grow back quickly. Besides—" he stood back to look her up and down, "you don't need your hair to be beautiful. It's your face. Your character shines through, and it makes you the most beautiful woman I've ever seen."

And she was. Her hair was short now, and she wore clothing from one of Amariah's sons—brown trousers and a shirt, with a heavy jacket over it. Her hair was wrapped in a kerchief, so as to hide what was left of it, but her large, dark eyes shone through, and George wondered how well the disguise would work. He leaned toward her, thinking to steal a kiss, but Amariah cleared his throat from behind them, indicating that he'd entered the room. George and Eliza jumped away from each other. "I don't mean to interrupt, but here's a mustache and beard. Dorcas made it herself." He took a couple of steps forward and pasted the facial hair to Eliza's face, quite completing the picture.

"Where did you get this?" Eliza asked, wrinkling her nose as the mustache tickled her.

"The children use it when they dress up as wise men for the Christmas play," Amariah laughed. "Though I must say it suits you quite well. No one would ever recognize you."

Dorcas walked in at that moment, carrying little Harry, and George laughed again to see his son dressed in girl's clothing, his pretty features completing the costume.

Eliza gave her husband a firm look. "George, isn't it time you dressed as well? We need to leave soon. Isn't that right?"

George nodded. "In only an hour, I've lost my family, adopted a husband, and found a daughter. I suppose you're right—it's time for me to change my identity as well."

Eliza picked up their child, grinning. "And what a pretty daughter he makes. What do you think, Harry, shall we call you Harriet?"

The boy looked at her, confused, and George laughed. "It'll take some gettin' used to, my dear. He recognizes your voice but not your face."

Harry, as if in answer, struggled to get out of Eliza's arms and reached for George. George took him up and turned to Dorcas. "And have you found us a guide, as you thought you might?"

The woman nodded. "One of the Negro women in my sewing group is going to escort Harry onto the boat in Sandusky and then travel to Canada with you. Her name is Constance Smyth. She is a short dark-skinned woman, who would never be mistaken for Eliza. Her traveling papers are genuine and in order already."

"Thank you," George answered, moving to the mirror on the wall. He took a few moments to spread some charcoal over his face, then turned back to the others. "And now, we're ready to go. Well disguised, if I do say so, as two men and a little girl. Why, we'll be safe in Canada in no time."

They filed from the room, their laughter dying down at the thought of moving forward in their journey. Now came the riskiest part, George knew, for they were going to be passing right under the noses of the slave catchers. Even disguised as they were, and with the plans he'd put in place, they wouldn't be safe until they were aboard the ship and setting off for Canada.

Outside, they found Amariah already in the wagon, ready to ride off. Jim and Anita stood to the side, their faces sorrowful.

"I can't talk you out of this, can I?" Jim asked quietly. "You know I believe it to be a trap. You can't trust that Loker, George. For all you know, he'll have men waitin' for you. For all you know, this is precisely what they'd already planned."

"Jim, my plan will work," George said firmly. "Our disguises are good. And they'll easily fool the slave catchers. Besides, I have a friend at hand to help—a plan that not even you know about. We'll be safe—I'm sure of it."

"And if you're wrong?"

"If Plan A doesn't work, we'll move on to Plan B."

"I'm even less confident in your Plan B," Jim noted wryly.

George turned to him and gave him a long, affectionate hug, then stood back and looked him in the eye. "Don't worry. We'll meet you in Montreal, just as we've planned. But hurry up, if you please. We'll need you to introduce us to the town!"

Jim laughed and shook his head at that, but let George go to join his family in Amariah's wagon. Then, with waves and calls of love, the wagon set off, leaving Jim, Anita, and Dorcas behind at the house.

~

They arrived at the wharf entrance several hours later, after a long, hard drive. It was a large wharf, with many buildings lining the small bay, and several ships at the dock. People roamed to and fro, both into and out of the buildings.

"Off with thee now," Amariah muttered. "I'll wait here until you're safely on the ship."

George clasped the man's shoulder. "Thank you for seein' us safely here, Amariah. I won't forget you for this."

"And for the money to get on the ship," Eliza added quickly. "We wouldn't be able to leave without you."

Amariah waved them off. "No need to thank me, friends. Just do the same for someone else, and all will be repaid. When you arrive in Canada, find Quakers. They'll help you get settled."

Mrs. Smyth picked up Harry, and Eliza and George jumped out of the wagon. They were dressed alike, in what looked to be worker uniforms, and both heavily smudged with charcoal. Eliza had her full mustache and beard. The disguises would work, George was sure of it. He picked up two large bags—actually just filled with pillows—and began to walk away from the wagon.

"Mrs. Smyth, you carry Harry ahead of us," he instructed. "We'll walk after you so that we don't look as though we're related. People must not associate Eliza and me with little Harriet."

As the four of them started forward, George found his eyes restlessly covering the wharf. There were men here to find them, he knew. Men who would want to capture them, and perhaps kill him. He had to be on alert.

It took him almost no time to spot them. Marks and Haley stood with their backs to the wall of a saloon, watching the passersby closely. They were pointing at some of them and speaking to each other, almost as if they were discussing who to go after. What they were really doing, George knew, was looking for him. He ducked farther into his jacket, hoping that the charcoal on his face was enough, and dropped a step behind Eliza.

Suddenly the two men darted forward and into their path, grabbing a black man and gesturing madly at him. George watched closely as the man fished in his vest for something and pulled out a set of papers. Despite the papers, they examined the right palm of the man. George's own right hand—wrapped up in rags, as though he'd been working in a factory—twinged, and he took a quick breath. They shouldn't approach them, but if they did—

"They're checking the Negroes they see," Eliza breathed next to him. "Oh George, what'll we do if they don't let us past?"

"Just keep walkin'," George muttered back. "Don't draw any attention to yourself. With these disguises, they'll never recognize us as runaways. Just keep walkin'."

Just then, George looked up to see Marks' eyes on him. The man was looking at him in wonderment, as if he couldn't believe what he was seeing. He turned and grabbed Haley's arm, and the other man turned to stare at George and his group as well.

George walked along, pretending to ignore them, but he could feel his body tightening with anger. If they came for him, he'd be ready, but he rather hoped they would just stay put.

"George, have faith," Eliza whispered. They walked quickly after Mrs. Smyth and their son toward the boat, each praying that Marks and Haley would stay in their place, or find some other Negroes to harass.

George could see the men turning to follow the group with their eyes. "Plan A isn't going to work," he whispered. "They're on to us."

"And Plan B?" Eliza answered fearfully.

George glanced around the wharf, beginning to doubt their safety himself. "Plan B should have happened by now. Something must be wrong. Perhaps he didn't get here as quickly as he meant to."

He glanced once over his shoulder and noted that Marks and Haley were getting closer to them. They were walking quickly now, and with purpose, Eliza and George their goal. Ahead of them, the ships reared up, but they hadn't reached the one they needed. Not yet. Within moments, they'd be trapped. He thought about going for his pistol, but before he could make a move, he heard a voice ringing out over the wharf.

"Hoy, Marks! Haley! I've got the darkies treed over here!" It was Loker, coming through with his part of the plan, and suddenly George's face broke out in a grin.

Haley and Marks both changed direction at the sound of his voice, moving off toward Loker. George spared them one glance, then turned back toward the boat, increasing his speed. This was their chance, and probably the only one they'd get. They needed to get on that boat, and quickly, before Haley and Marks realized that they'd been fooled. He didn't know what Loker would actually do to them, but they'd see soon enough that he didn't, in fact, have any darkies at all.

Mrs. Smyth was already ahead of them, handing money to a man George assumed must be Gene. The man counted the money, then looked up and nodded.

"Negro cabin's near the back," he said roughly. "Suggest you get there quick as you can, while those slave traders that was followin' you are takin' care of other business."

George, Eliza, and Mrs. Smyth hurried onto the boat without answering.

∼

Free, they were nearly free, if only this boat would hurry up and leave. George was standing on the deck, looking back toward the wharf. There was no sign of Marks, Haley, or Loker, and he wondered briefly what Loker had told the other two.

He just hoped it was enough to keep them absent for a while longer.

"I wish this boat would embark," he muttered to the worker standing next to him.

"Soon, dear," Eliza answered, watching the wharf as well.

A moment later, the bell rung out, and the men on the wharf began untying the ship. Then, with a great amount of shouting, they shoved at it, pushing it away from the dock and onto the water. Suddenly new shouts rang out across the dock, and George looked up to see Marks and Haley running toward them, screaming for the boat to stop. But it had already embarked, and the two slave catchers came to a halt at the edge of the planking, to stare helplessly after the vessel.

George and Eliza, grinning with their freedom, waved gaily at the two men who had tried to catch them. Marks and Haley scowled and shouted but could do nothing, and finally George turned to Eliza and took her in his arms.

Others might be wondering why he was hugging another man so fondly, but he didn't care. He took a deep breath, spun her around, and looked out over Lake Erie. The water was just turning blue in the coming dawn, and he thought he'd never seen anything quite so beautiful. It was the first time he'd allowed himself to truly feel free, and it was unlike anything he'd ever felt. Beyond that, it was something that every man should be able to feel for himself.

"One, day, Eliza," he said quietly, "I'll come back here, and I'll help as many Negroes as I can get to safety, and to freedom. God's given me my own life, and I want to use it helpin' others to find theirs."

CHAPTER 40

George stretched out on the blanket, blissfully happy. Above him, Eliza was busy dishing out the food she'd packed, muttering to Anita about the price of decent ham. George smiled, then turned his eyes to the trees above him and the birds on the branches. Montreal was far more beautiful than he'd ever imagined, the air sweeter here, the birds more tuneful. Though he thought he was probably biased.

He was, after all, a free man here.

"What a beautiful day," he murmured.

"It is a wonderful day, isn't it?" Eliza answered. She put a hand out toward their son. "Harry, don't eat all the biscuits. I don't think Jim's even had one yet."

"But Mamma, Granny Anita said Jim ate these biscuits as a

boy, to get so big and strong. And I want to be big and strong, just like him."

"Boy, don't try to grow up too fast. Bein' a man isn't all fun and games," Jim said, chuckling.

"Let the boy eat! He's growin', needs his food," Anita joined in.

"Anita, you'll spoil him," Eliza scolded.

Finally George sat up, ready to join the conversation. "Isn't that what grandmothers are for? I've never had one, myself, but I've always heard it's their callin' in life. Besides, these biscuits are almost as good as Aunt Chloe's. I don't blame the boy for wantin' more of them."

Eliza sighed. "Poor Aunt Chloe, I wonder how she's doin' with Uncle Tom sold off."

George reached for her. "Not well, I expect."

"I don't know what I'd do if I ever lost you like that, George."

He kissed her gently on the brow. "Well you'll never have to worry about it, my dear. We're in Canada now, free as the birds above, and you'll never lose me." Suddenly he jerked, memory returning, and glanced at the timepiece on his vest. "And speakin' of free men, I must get back to the machinist shop. They're expectin' me to work on a new gadget they've brought in from Europe."

"Papa, do you have to go?" Harry asked plaintively.

George reached over and ruffled the boy's hair. "I have to go and make money to buy the flour that makes your biscuits, boy. But don't worry, I'll be home in a few hours."

Eliza caught his hand, giving him one last kiss. "George, do you ever think about the people we left behind? Those on the Harris plantation, and the Shelby place? I almost feel bad livin' such a good life when they're there, sufferin'."

George laughed. "Eliza, I wouldn't worry too much about the Harris slaves. I have a feeling someone's goin' to come along and save them from Harris' tyranny any day now."

Eliza frowned. "How do you know?"

George looked up at Jim and winked. Jim gave him a slow grin and winked back. Eliza watched the two of them suspiciously, her eyes narrowing.

"And what was that? What are the two of you plannin' now?"

"We aren't plannin' anything, Eliza," George answered softly. "We're simply followin' God's plan. And it's a good one."

Chloe was lying on the pallet, her heart sinking lower and lower. Tom lay behind her, his arms around her waist. Outside, full night had fallen, though the light from the moon was full and bright, coming through the window to illuminate the small, shabby room around them. She could hear her husband breathing softly behind her, and her three children on their pallets on the other side of the room, their soft snorts and grumblings telling her that they were well and truly asleep.

She pushed back against Tom, reveling for a moment in the feeling of his arms around her. He'd always made her feel secure. Safe, no matter what was going on around them. And now...

She was supposed to be asleep, she knew. But she couldn't sleep. Didn't want to sleep. For Tom was leaving—being sent away, sold by their master—and she didn't know if she'd ever see him again. What was one night of sleeplessness in the face of an eternity apart?

It had been several days since they'd learned from Eliza that Master Shelby had sold Tom and young Harry to the slave trader, Haley, to be sent far from their homes. Haley himself had been there the morning after Eliza, notifying them of the same, his sly grin sending chills up and down Chloe's spine.

Then the master and Haley had found that Eliza had run away—as Tom and Chloe had already known—and Haley had run off into the wilds in search of the girl and her son.

Chloe and Tom had spent every night after that taking as much joy as they could in each other, storing up a lifetime's worth of memories together. She had forgotten how Tom had been as a younger man—before the children, before he found Jesus. The past few nights had been more passionate than the nights just after they had jumped over the broom, and they had been wonderful.

Not tonight. Tonight Tom had just wanted to hold her against him, breathing in her scent and memorizing the feel of her body. As if he knew that their time together was drawing to a close.

"Tom, you awake?" she asked, suddenly needing to hear his voice.

He grunted. "How can I sleep, woman, when I can almost hear the worryin' goin' on in your head?"

"Aren't you worried?" she hissed, frustrated.

"And what should I worry about?" he asked affectionately. "I have all the things I need right now—you in my arms and my children sleepin' sound across the cabin."

She paused, then voiced her darkest fear. "What if Haley comes back tomorrow?"

"He does, guess I'll be goin' with him," Tom answered quietly.

"How can you go somewhere when you don't know where you're goin'? I wish you'd run with Lizzie and her boy. Least then I'd know you were safe."

Tom squeezed her firmly, "And if I had, Mas'r Shelby might've been forced to sell the four of you to different plantations. How would I ever find you if he did that?"

Chloe nearly sobbed. "Find us? What makes you think you'll ever be free to go lookin'?"

"But if I am, Chloe, won't it be easier to find you if you're all together? Let's not worry about tomorrow's trouble. Just let me enjoy my beautiful wife."

Chloe grew quiet, his words bringing her some peace. He was right, she knew—if he was free, finding the four of them would be easier if they were here, at the Shelby plantation.

Deep in her heart though, in a place that didn't require any words, she wondered if that would ever happen.

~

C hloe awoke to a pounding on the door that might have woken the dead. Her eyes flew around the room, seeking and then finding her three children. They were still abed, their fuzzy heads lined up on the pillow like cotton balls. The small fireplace held nothing but the remains of last night's fire, and in front of it sat the pot she'd used for the stew the night before. The small window was barely light, telling her that it was just past dawn, if the sun had risen at all.

Everything here was the same as it had been the night before, but the pounding at the door told her that things were about to change.

Tom grunted and stood, grabbing his trousers as he headed

for the door. By the time he got there, the door was already swinging open.

"Let's go, boy, get your things and get to the driveway."

The voice was loud and uncultured, and Chloe didn't have to guess at who it was. Master Shelby would never have spoken to any of them that way.

Haley had returned. And he was taking her husband.

"Just let me say g'bye to my family, Mas'r Haley, and then I'll come," Tom muttered, looking down at his feet.

"Well hurry it up! I ain't got all day!" the man returned. "Yon girl's already cost me enough time as it is, don't mean to take no trouble with you as well."

Chloe was up and shrugging into her dress when her husband returned. Her sons Pete and Mose were on their feet as well, rubbing their eyes in confusion. Polly, the youngest, was awake and sitting up on her pallet, as if waiting for someone to pick her up. Chloe rushed to the child and gathered her into her arms. Then, without words, the family gathered in the middle of the room.

Tom looked toward the boys. "Now boys, your pa has to go away. We've spoken 'bout this. You must do everything your ma asks you to do. She speaks for us both now."

"Yes, Pa," the boys answered in unison.

"And do what Mas'r and Missis Shelby ask you to do. Don't give them any reason to dislike you."

"Yes, Pa."

Tom reached out and took Polly from Chloe's arms. He turned her face toward his and kissed her lightly on the nose. "Polly, I pray you'll grow up to be just as pretty as your ma and cook half as well as she does. Do that and Mas'r Shelby won't never sell you."

Chloe wiped the tears from her eyes, her heart breaking. "I would die before I let them sell her," she murmured.

Tom handed the baby back to her and took her in his arms. "Never say that," he whispered. "For you must be alive when I return. You must be waitin' for me, and ready to run." He kissed her soundly on the lips, then stood back and gazed at his family. "This is how I'll see you any time I close my eyes," he said quietly, tears streaming down his cheeks.

Then he turned and picked up the rough hemp bag he'd packed several days earlier and headed for the door. The family followed, stumbling slightly in their shock, and gathered in the open doorway.

Outside, the sun had barely risen above the horizon, but Chloe could see the plantation in the dim lighting. The big house stood directly across from their cabin, with the barn on the other side of it. Behind her, she knew, the other cabins stretched toward the fields, the homes of many just like her—people who had no control over their own lives, or those of their loved ones.

Then, to her surprise, she saw Mrs. Shelby dashing toward them from the main house. Chloe watched her, confused; what did the woman think she was doing? She couldn't stop what was happening here. Mr. Shelby had already signed the papers. Still, at least she cared enough to come say good-bye to Tom. Not like Master Shelby, who was obviously too embarrassed to witness what he'd done.

Mrs. Shelby reached Haley in the driveway and took him by the arm, speaking earnestly up at him. Chloe wasn't close enough to hear what she was saying over her children's cries, but she could see that her mistress's face was flushed with emotion, her eyes glassy.

She glanced at her husband and saw him turn to her and speak. Something must have been wrong though, for she couldn't hear what he said either.

Now Haley brushed Mrs. Shelby off and turned abruptly toward Tom, gesturing toward the wagon. Tom heaved a sigh and walked slowly along with his new master, stopping only when he drew even with the wagon. Haley laughed—

Chloe could see that much—and bent down to fix two heavy shackles to her Tom's ankles. Tom closed his eyes in pain and regret but climbed into the back of the wagon and took a seat. He turned back to his family and gave them one last wave, and then the wagon was drawing away, out the gate and onto the road.

Chloe watched the wagon until she couldn't even see its dust anymore. Then her hearing seemed to return, and she realized she was surrounded by the sound of sobbing. Her children were crying, and the slaves of the plantation stood around her, all of them sniffing and crying. She turned and saw that Mrs. Shelby was drawing toward her, no doubt to comfort her in this time of sorrow.

But Chloe turned and stalked back into her cabin. Mrs. Shelby might not have been the one who sold Tom, but she'd certainly known about it. And for that, Chloe would never forgive her.

Besides, she had breakfast to cook, for her own family and the families of the plantation. At the moment, that was easier than dwelling on what had just happened.

~

The kitchen in the main house was larger than her own, of course, but Chloe didn't want to leave her home yet. She started the fire at the stove and began to grease the pan, getting ready to make griddle cakes. As she worked, she allowed her thoughts to wander. She was angry at Haley, who had taken her husband, but she was angrier at Master Shelby. Tom had been on the Shelby plantation since he was born and had always been faithful to the family. He'd worked more than double his worth. Shelby should have freed him long ago and had, in fact, promised Tom his freedom the year before. With his freedom, Tom had planned to work and buy his family from the Shelbys. Eventually, they would have all been free. But now...

Suddenly she felt someone grab her from behind. She spun around to see Pete, his face shocked.

"What is it?" she gasped. "Has something happened? Did Tom come back?"

"No, Ma, the stove's on fire," he snapped, pointing.

Chloe turned to see flames leaping from the stove, licking up from the door of the oven as if they would devour it. She took several steps back, surprised, and turned back to Pete, who led her out of the cabin. There she found her children, as well as many of the other slaves. Spinning back toward the cabin, she saw that the flames had already spread to the dry wood of the walls and the straw of the roof. In a matter of moments, the entire cabin was aflame, along with everything in it.

Then Mr. Shelby was at her side, breathing heavily.

Now he comes, now that Tom is gone, she thought, furious.

"Is there anyone inside?" Mr. Shelby asked, huffing.

"No, Mas'r," Chloe answered quietly.

"And why is no one getting any water?" he asked, shocked. No one answered, and he turned to the crowd. "Someone get some water!" he shouted. "We must put this out, or the entire place will go up in flames!"

At his words, the slaves—angry at the fact that he'd sold Tom—finally began to move, though they didn't answer him. Mr. Shelby turned to Chloe and met her eyes for the first time, staring deeply into them. Chloe looked back, unwilling to back down, and put all her anger and frustration and sorrow into that one look. Finally he turned away, dropping his eyes.

Chloe watched him walk away, then turned back to her cabin. The roof was well lit now, and raging, the flames popping and crackling as they tore through the dry straw. The walls still stood, but she didn't think they'd stand for much longer, though they were built of stronger stuff than the roof.

God alone knew what was going on inside the cabin itself. She closed her eyes and prayed. Not for their cabin, or their meager possessions. Those were just physical signs of the fire burning away at her heart, the physical burning of what her life had been. No, she prayed that God would send someone to save her husband from his life as a slave so that he might come back and save her and the children.

So that they might be a family again one day, in a place where they were free to live without worrying about whether someone else might send them away for no reason.

GET YOUR FREE STORY!

Go to the link below and get your free copy of the story, *The Runaway Slave Returns*. It's a prequel to *Burning Uncle Tom's Cabin*.

www.BrightSons.com/RSRFree

DID YOU ENJOY THE STORY?

Thank you so much for taking the time to read our story. It would mean a lot to us if you could post a review of the book on Amazon, telling future readers what you liked.

Leaving a review will only take a minute and the review can be as short as you like. Reviews are very important, but few readers leave them. Please help us out by being the exception.

Click on the link below to post your review.

www.BrightSons.com/BUTCReview

Carl Waters

Carl Waters, born and raised in Atlanta, Georgia, grew up reading comic books and dreamed of being a new kind of superhero. Waters never forgot his childhood dreams, which over the years transformed into a desire to create new heroes, particularly African-American male heroes, through writing.

Kalvin C. Chinyere, MD, MBA

Kalvin Chinedu Chinyere, fondly known as Dr. Kal, was born in Miami, Florida, to immigrant parents. His Jamaican mother and Nigerian father raised him in Miami and in Queens, New York.

Dr. Kal started high school at the Bronx High School of Science in New York, then graduated from Miami North-western Senior High School in Florida. He later attended the University of Miami, where he became a brother of Omega Psi Phi Fraternity, Inc. and received both his Bachelor of Science and Doctor of Medicine degrees. Dr. Kal then received his Master of Business Administration from Emory University's Goizueta School of Business.

Dr. Kal lives in Atlanta, Georgia, where he's a full-time

Internal Medicine physician. He is also the father of the most beautiful little girl to ever walk the face of this planet.

In his spare time, Dr. Kal started Bright Sons Media, LLC. He and his company are dedicated to creating media that accurately portrays African-Americans by removing the negative images and false stereotypes found throughout mainstream media.

Bright Sons' first release was the novel, Burning Uncle Tom's Cabin, which reimagines Harriet Beecher Stowe's classic tale. Their most recent project is Black to the Future, with the goal of increasing all forms of wealth in the Black community.

Made in the USA
Middletown, DE
14 October 2018